ACPL ITEM

S0-DSD-222

The bearer of this scroll, namely,

is a wizard of the Shianti

# THE WORLD of LONE WOLF
# PAGE AND DEVER

### The Author

IAN PAGE was born in London in 1960. Since the age of sixteen he has pursued a successful career as a singer/songwriter. With the band *Secret Affair*, he had a string of chart hits to his credit including 'Time for Action' and 'My World'. His interest in the fantastic worlds of 'Sword and Sorcery' dates back to his early teens, and to his love of the novels of J. R. R. Tolkien and Michael Moorcock. It was in 1979, when Joe Dever introduced him to role-playing games, that his involvement in the world of Magnamund began. He has since contributed greatly to the development of the southern reaches of this fantastic world, and has worked closely with Joe on several other role-playing games projects that include TV and radio appearances.

### The Editor

JOE DEVER was born in 1956 at Woodford Bridge in Essex. His involvement with role-playing games dates back to 1977 when, on a trip to Los Angeles, he discovered 'Dungeons and Dragons'. In 1982 he won the Advanced Dungeons and Dragons Championships in America, where he was the only British competitor. His bestselling Lone Wolf adventures (available in Beaver Books) are the culmination of many years of developing the world of Magnamund. Printed in several languages and sold throughout the world, they have earned both him and co-author Gary Chalk recognition as masters of the gamebook craft. Joe Dever also writes for modelling journals, is a contributing editor to *White Dwarf*—Britain's leading role-playing games magazine, adapts the Lone Wolf adventures for computer play and is noted for his model photography. Together with Gary Chalk, he produces the Lone Wolf Club Newsletter and enjoys answering letters from readers all over the world.

The *LONE WOLF* Series
from Berkley/Pacer

The *WORLD OF LONE WOLF* Series

THE MAGNAMUND COMPANION:
The Complete Guide to the World
of Lone Wolf and Grey Star

The *FREEWAY WARRIOR* Series

# THE WORLD OF LONE WOLF

**BOOK 4**

# War Of the Wizards

**Written by Ian Page**
**Edited by Joe Dever**
**Illustrated by Paul Bonner**

*Pacer* BOOKS FOR YOUNG ADULTS

**B**

BERKLEY BOOKS, NEW YORK

This Berkley/Pacer book contains the complete
text of the original hardcover edition.

WAR OF THE WIZARDS

A Berkley/Pacer Book / published by arrangement with
Century Hutchinson Limited

PRINTING HISTORY
Beaver Books edition published 1986
Berkley/Pacer edition / November 1987

All rights reserved.
Concept © Joe Dever and Gary Chalk 1986
Text © Ian Page 1986
Illustrations © Century Hutchinson Ltd. 1986
This book may not be reproduced in whole or in part,
by mimeograph or any other means, without permission.
For information address: Century Hutchinson Limited,
Brookmount House, 62-65 Chandos Place,
London WC2N 4NW England

ISBN: 0-425-10539-3

A BERKLEY BOOK ® TM 757,375
Berkley/Pacer Books are published by The Berkley Publishing Group,
200 Madison Avenue, New York, NY 10016.
The name "BERKLEY" and the "B" logo
are trademarks belonging to Berkley Publishing Corporation.

PRINTED IN THE UNITED STATES OF AMERICA

10    9    8    7    6    5    4

*To Alison*

# ACTION CHART

## LESSER MAGICKS

| | |
|---|---|
| 1 | ~~sorcery~~ ~~alchemy~~ Alchemy |
| 2 | ~~enchantment~~ PROPHECY |
| 3 | ~~elementalism~~ ENCHANTMENT |
| 4 | ~~prophecy~~ Elementalism |
| 5 | ~~psychomancy~~ SORCERY |
| 6 | ~~evocation~~ |

If completed any previous World of Lone Wolf adventures

## HIGHER MAGICKS

| | |
|---|---|
| 1 | ~~thaumaturgy~~ Theurgy |
| 2 | ~~theurgy~~ Necromancy |
| 3 | ~~physiurgy~~ Telergy |
| 4 | ~~theurgy~~ Physiurgy |
| 5 | ~~visionary~~ Thaumaturgy |
| 6 | ~~necromancy~~ |

If completed any previous World of Lone Wolf adventures

## HERB POUCH (Maximum 6 articles)

| | |
|---|---|
| 1 | ~~vait~~ |
| 2 | ~~vait~~ Enchantment potion |
| 3 | ~~saltpetre~~ OLAMSPUI |
| 4 | ~~saltpetre~~ 6EP |
| 5 | LAWMSPUI = 4ED |
| 6 | ALEfHER = 2CS |

Only carried if you possess
Magical Power of Alchemy

## MEALS

4 3

(Carried in Backpack)
– 3 EP if no Meals available
when instructed to eat

## BELT POUCH
containing Nobles (50 maximum)

2 tamara seeds and willpower

| COMBAT SKILL | WILLPOWER | ENDURANCE POINTS |
|---|---|---|
| 18¹⁸ | 80 44 57 | 5 36 4 |
| | May go above Initial Score | Can never go above Initial Score   0 = dead |

# COMBAT RECORD

| ENDURANCE POINTS | WILLPOWER POINTS | | ENDURANCE POINTS |
|---|---|---|---|
| GREY STAR | | COMBAT RATIO | ENEMY |
| 30 | 0 | 0 | 19 1 |
| GREY STAR | | COMBAT RATIO | ENEMY |
| 29 | 5 | -14 | 40 |
| GREY STAR | | COMBAT RATIO | ENEMY |
| | 8 | | |
| GREY STAR | | COMBAT RATIO | ENEMY |
| | | | |
| GREY STAR | | COMBAT RATIO | ENEMY |
| | | | |
| GREY STAR | | COMBAT RATIO | ENEMY |
| | | | |

# SPECIAL ITEMS

| DESCRIPTION | KNOWN EFFECTS |
|---|---|
| Map | |
| MASBATE BATTLE HORN | |

## BACKPACK ITEMS

- Meal
- Meal
- Meal
- ~~Meat~~ Water Bottle
- Moonstone Touch
- Tinder box
- Rope
- Touch

Can be discarded when not in combat

## WEAPONS (maximum 2 Weapons, Wizard's Staff counts as 1 Weapon)

1. Wizard Staff
2. Spear

If combat entered without Wizard's Staff − 6 CS.
If combat entered without a Weapon − 8 CS.

CS = Combat Skill        EP = Endurance

# OF THE COMING OF GREY STAR

Ancient days they were when first the Shianti set foot upon the land that men call Magnamund. Long had they journeyed through the void, homeless wanderers in search of a place to call their own. And so it was that when the Shianti first looked upon the face of the land, their hearts were raised in wonder. They saw a world of nameless mountains, untamed forests and lands both wild and free. Here they chose to cease their wanderings and to devote themselves to the study and appreciation of this new found land.

To the delight of the Shianti, the race of man first emerged at this time and they watched his early struggle towards civilization with eager concern. Like gods, the Shianti seemed to the minds of primitive men. Tall and proud, shining with a radiance that spoke of magic and arcane mystery, the Shianti moved among them and with their powers of wizardry, aided man in his development.

As the centuries passed, man fell to worship of the magicial Shianti and the power of these wizards grew even stronger. With hungry hearts they sought to unlock the mysteries of knowledge, sending their minds into other planes of existence and strange worlds beyond the sphere of the material plane. Their foresight was now unmatched and the power of their thought was mighty indeed. It was at this time that they created the Moonstone. Woven of the very fabric of the astral plane of Daziarn, this translucent gem was the greatest achievement of Shianti wisdom. It was the binding force of all Shianti magic, containing the combined might of all their wizardry, the sum of all their knowledge. The Golden Age of the Shianti had come and the Moonstone was the instrument of their dominion throughout all Magnamund. Man stood as little more than a shadow, blinded by the shining white light of Shianti glory. But, in creating the Moonstone, the unwritten laws of nature had been transgressed. For the Moonstone, like the Shianti themselves, was something outside of man's own world; it defied the natural order laid down by the creators of the Earth and disrupted the balance that the gods had designed.

The Goddess Ishir, High Priestess of the Moon and mother of all men, showed herself to the Shianti and spoke to them of the destiny of man: 'The children of this world must claim their inheritance. Their time has come and they must learn to stand alone. They are lost in their worship of you and the day draws ever nearer when they will covet the power of the Moonstone.'

And the Shianti said: 'Forgive us, Great Goddess, for we intend no harm. We love mankind even as you do. We have sought to do good and protect your children from harm.'

But Ishir replied, 'Of this there can be no doubt, but this world is not your realm. Man must be free to pursue his destiny alone, and you must leave, for you trespass on his domain.'

The Shianti were filled with sorrow. They feared a

return to the void and to their lonely wandering, and pleaded with Ishir that she might allow them to remain. Ishir was filled with pity for them. She spoke again, saying, 'If you are to remain you must obey my command. You must take a vow never to interfere with mankind's fate. As a token of good faith you must lay aside the Moonstone, and return it to the plane where it belongs.'

Solemnly, the Shianti agreed. The vow was sworn before Ishir, and the Moonstone was returned to the Daziarn. The Shianti abandoned their cities and moved south to the Isle of Lorn. They encircled their new home with a web of enchantments, magical mists and mage winds to prevent man from ever finding their place of refuge in the Sea of Dreams. Knowledge of the Shianti faded with time, save in southern Magnamund where it became enshrined in legend, and the worship of them endured. Priests of the Shianti religion preserved their lore and patiently awaited the day when the 'ancient ones' would return, bringing with them lasting peace and the blessing of a new golden age.

Two thousand years strode by and man advanced as Ishir had foretold. He built great cities and cultivated the land; his kingdoms rose and fell; he made war and loved and laughed and became master of his fate. But a new power arose in the province of Shadaki. There Shasarak the evil Wytch-king ruled. The black necromancer commanded an army of brutal soldiers and had a devoted following of men who upheld his religion of demonic worship and sacrificial rites. Devotees of the Shianti and other religious cults were persecuted in a merciless purge. Ruthlessly, the

11

Wytch-king destroyed all his opponents and began a terrible war with the peoples of the neighbouring provinces. From the ruins of war Shasarak shaped the Shadakine Empire, subjugating whole nations to his evil rule. And, as the provinces fell to his might, the Shianti looked on helplessly, bound by their vow to the Goddess Ishir never to interfere in the affairs of man.

On the night of the crowning of Shasarak as Overlord of the Shadakine Empire, a great storm broke upon the Sea of Dreams, a storm that raged with unnatural intensity. Lashed by wind and rain, illuminated by wild lightning, the waters heaved and danced in fury to the thundering music of the storm, unchecked by even the enchantments of the Shianti. When finally the tempest died, the Shianti looked out in amazement on the shattered hull of a ship drifting towards their shore. Never before had this occurred, for the enchantments and mage winds had kept them secure from the curiosity of man by forcing him to sail close to his own land.

The Shianti went quickly to the ruined ship where they found only one survivor – a baby. They perceived the sudden arrival of this human child as a sign of great portent, and they conceived a plan by which they might lawfully aid mankind. They named the orphan child Grey Star because a star is the symbol of hope in the Shianti faith, and because of the silver streak in the child's jet-black hair. In the shadow of the wrath of the Goddess Ishir, they raised the child as one of their own and taught him their secrets. Diligently they set about their instruction, for their aim was to provide a saviour for mankind. Armed with the might of Shianti wizardry and wisdom, their hope was to create an adversary equal in power to the evil Wytch-king of Shadaki, for they realized that only with the death of Shasarak would man once more be free to determine his destiny.

# THE STORY SO FAR...

You are Grey Star, trained in the ancient lore of a Shianti wizard. For sixteen years you have dwelt in safety on the Isle of Lorn, the hidden realm of the magical Shianti race, until Acarya, High Wizard of the Shianti, sent you upon a dangerous quest to save your people, the race of man, from the evil rule of Shasarak, the tyrannical Wytch-king of the Shadakine Empire. Held by their ancient vow to the Goddess Ishir, the Shianti are unable to leave their island and come to the aid of man themselves but no such promise prohibited you from leaving the island and you were sent to recover the Moonstone and use its power to defeat the Wytch-king.

The Moonstone, an artefact that possesses the combined force of all Shianti wisdom and power, was hidden on the Daziarn plane and you first had to find the invisible gateway to the Daziarn, the Shadow Gate. To help you find the Gate, you sought the Lost Tribe of Lara, a race of magical but primitive creatures called the Kundi, who possess the gift of astral vision, enabling them to see magic portals and gateways to other planes and dimensions. When Shasarak's Shadakine army first invaded the free provinces of the south, they came through the forests of the Mountains of Lara where the Kundi lived, and were constantly ambushed and delayed by the Kundi. The Kundi always eluded them, disappearing into the dense forest before the Shadakine could retaliate and, finally, in wrath, the Wytch-king burnt down the forests and forced the Kundi to flee south. No one knew where they came to rest.

Voyaging across the Sea of Dreams, you came first to the city of Suhn, the largest port in the Shadakine Empire. There you were befriended by a cheerful merchant named Shan Li, a widely travelled man. Your questions about the Lost Tribe aroused suspicion in Suhn and you were captured and taken to the House of Correction, the prison of Suhn, and subjected to the truthsay of Mother Magri, Shadakine Wytch and Law-giver. With the aid of the power of the Kazim Stone, she attempted to read your mind, but you were able to preserve the secret of your quest.

With the help of Tanith, a young and beautiful girl learning the ways of wytchcraft in the service of Mother Magri, you were able to escape from the House of Correction. With Shan as your guide, you eventually turned south and headed towards the region known as the Azanam, for it seemed likely that the Lost Tribe had settled there. However, again using the power of the Kazim Stone, Mother Magri summoned a Kleasá against you – a demon shadow that feeds upon the soul. Neither your Magical Powers, nor the might of your Wizard's Staff were

14

able to defeat the Kleasá, and it had almost destroyed you when Tanith cast a spell and called the demon against herself. She was totally consumed by the Kleasá and both disappeared in flames. Her brave sacrifice saved your life.

At the Azanam you found the Kundi and they gave you their Shaman, Urik the Wise, to guide you to the Shadow Gate. You travelled across the hostile lands of the Shadakine Empire and, close to the gates of the city of Karnali, you freed a man named Samu, a former king of the extinct tribe of the Masbaté, from a Shadakine slave train. Then the leader of the rebel Freedom Guild, Sado of the Long Knife, enlisted your aid in freeing the city of Karnali from the rule of its Shadakine Wytch and her warriors, but you did not, for still you had to find the Shadow Gate. You journeyed on, accompanied by Samu, Urik, and a thief by the name of Hugi. On this later stage of your journey, you discovered that Shasarak was once a Shianti Master. So now you know your eventual confrontation will be with one versed in the same magical arts as yourself. You finally found the Shadow Gate beneath the wasteland of Desolation Valley, only to discover that the magic portal was guarded by a demon Kleasá, holding in its grasp Tanith, who had not after all been slain in her attempt to save you. Instead, the Kleasá had offered her to its master, Shasarak, as a prisoner. Using Tanith as a shield, the Kleasá withstood your attempts to gain entry to the Daziarn portal but, at last you managed to force the Kleasá away from the Shadow Gate and stepped through to be reunited with Tanith.

Together you entered the Daziarn plane which held

many mysteries and perils, the worst of which was the Jahksa, a creature created in your likeness by Shasarak. You travelled through this strange, abstract world until, at last, you came to the Trianon, a chamber floating in the void. Within the Trianon was the Moonstone and, after a last paradoxical confrontation with the Jahksa in which the lawful and magical effects of the Moonstone were used, the Jahksa was defeated and the Moonstone made yours.

With the Moonstone now resting in your hand, you begin the final part of your quest to defeat the Wytchking. Armed with the might of the Moonstone, you now possess the only known power that can destroy Shasarak the renegade Shianti Wizard.


# THE GAME RULES


To keep a record of your adventure, use the *Action Chart* at the front of this book. If you run out of space, you can copy out the chart or have it photocopied.

Before you set off on your adventure, you must discover how well your Shianti masters have prepared you for your quest by determining your fighting prowess – COMBAT SKILL – your state of mind – WILLPOWER– and your physical stamina – ENDURANCE.

To do this, take a pencil and, with eyes closed, point with the blunt end of it on to the *Random Number Table* on the last page of this book. If you pick *0* it counts as *zero*.

The first number that you pick from the *Random Number Table* in this way represents your COMBAT SKILL. Add 10 to the number you picked and write the total in the COMBAT SKILL section of your *Action Chart* (eg, if your pencil fell on the number 4 in the *Random Number Table* you would write in a COMBAT SKILL of 14). When you fight, your COMBAT SKILL will be pitted against that of your enemy. A high score in this section is therefore very desirable.

The second number that you need is one to represent your WILLPOWER. Do not use the *Random Number Table*. You begin this adventure with a WILLPOWER total of 50, as your first touch of the Moonstone of the Shianti regenerates your Magical Powers immediately. If you possess unused WILLPOWER points from earlier Grey Star adventures, add them to the 50 WILLPOWER points which possession of the Moonstone grants you. Write the total in the WILLPOWER section of your *Action Chart*. If you decide to use a spell or the power of your Wizard's Staff, then you will lose WILLPOWER points. If at any time your WILLPOWER falls to zero, or below, you may not use any spells or any additional WILLPOWER points in combat to increase the ENDURANCE loss of an opponent. Lost WILLPOWER points can be regained during the course of the adventure and it is possible for your WILLPOWER score to rise above the total with which you start your adventure.

The third attribute is your power of ENDURANCE. You start with a total of 30 ENDURANCE points when your first touch of the Moonstone fills your body with energy and power. Add any ENDURANCE points gained from playing previous Grey Star adventures to your initial score of 30 and write the total in the ENDURANCE section of your *Action Chart*. If you are wounded in combat, you will lose ENDURANCE points. If at any time your ENDURANCE score falls to zero, you are dead and the adventure is over. Lost ENDURANCE points can be regained during the course of the adventure but can never rise above the number with which you began the adventure.

## MAGICAL POWERS

There are thirteen Magical Powers, the first seven of which are called the *lesser magicks*. Possession of the Moonstone reveals to you the secret of the magical powers known as the *higher magicks*, of which there are six. If this is your first Grey Star adventure, you may choose five lesser magicks and four higher magicks. If you have successfully completed any of the previous Grey Star adventures, you may choose six lesser magicks and five higher magicks.

The Magical Powers available to you are listed below. When you have chosen your powers enter them in the Magical Powers section of your *Action Chart.*

This power allows a wizard to transform his thoughts or desires into magical energy. By concentration of the will it is possible to create magical shields of force to bar doors or move objects. Sorcery drains more WILLPOWER points than any other Magical Power, and is most effective when your WILLPOWER points are high.

If you choose this power, write 'Sorcery' on your *Action Chart*.

The power of Enchantment enables a wizard to charm or beguile other creatures, and create illusions in the minds of others. He will be able to extract information from others, place thoughts and compulsions into another's mind or cause them to believe that imaginary events are actually taking place. Some magical or highly intelligent beings may be immune to the powers of Enchantment.

If you choose this power, write 'Enchantment' on your *Action Chart*.

The power of elemental magic allows a wizard some control over the natural elements of Air, Fire, Earth, and Water. By entering a trance and chanting incantations, you may summon aid from the spirits of the Elemental plane. Elementals have very little understanding of man, and for this reason a wizard can never be sure of the nature of the aid the Elementals may send.

If you choose this power, write 'Elementalism' on your *Action Chart*.

# Alchemy

A wizard who possesses the power of Alchemy is able, through the mixing of various substances, to create magical potions. Given the correct ingredients, a potion may restore lost energy (ie, ENDURANCE points, WILLPOWER), or temporarily improve various abilities (eg, COMBAT SKILL). The use of alchemy may also allow a wizard to alter the nature of substances (eg, change lead into gold), but the necessary ingredients and the correct equipment (eg, a pestle and mortar) must be at hand. The use of the power of Alchemy drains no WILLPOWER

If you choose this power write 'Alchemy' on your *Action Chart*.

# PROPHECY

The power of prophecy allows a wizard to foretell the future through meditation. A meditative state will allow a wizard to make the correct decision when facing conflicting choices or difficult actions; to discover the whereabouts of a person he has once met, or an object he has once seen. It may also allow him to determine the true nature of a stranger or a strange object. Magical beings or objects are sometimes hidden from the power of divination.

If you choose this power, write 'Prophecy' on your *Action Chart*.

This power bestows upon a wizard the ability to deduce facts about events by touching objects connected to them. Through deep concentration, a wizard may lay his hands upon any inanimate object and visualize scenes that have affected it. Visions brought about through the use of Psychomancy are often cryptic, taking the form of a riddle or puzzle. Some magic items are resistant to the use of Psychomancy and may, sometimes, impart misleading information.

If you choose this power, write 'Psychomancy' on your *Action Chart*.

# EVOCATION

Mastery of this power permits contact with the spirit realm. A wizard wishing to speak with the dead, or to call up a form from the spirit world, must draw a magic pentacle and enter a trance, when the use of the correct spell-chant will reach out to the Spiritual plane. Standing within the protection of a magic pentacle, a wizard may consider himself to be relatively safe from harm. If he wishes to speak with a corpse, especially one whose former life was good and righteous, then a wizard can expect help and advice. However, contact with those whose former lives were evil or selfish can be a perilous, and often fatal, experience. Evil spirits are reluctant to return to the realm of the dead and may try to trick a wizard into freeing them into the world of the living. All spirits, good and evil, will require some service of the wizard in return for their aid. Any failure to perform this task, however difficult, may result in the wizard losing his life.

If you choose this power, write 'Evocation' on your *Action Chart*.

This higher magick is an advanced form of Sorcery, the craft of magical energy. Where Sorcery allows a wizard to affect external things, Thaumaturgy affects the wizard himself. The power of Thaumaturgy can bestow upon a wizard the power of levitation, a limited form of flying; invulnerability and increased strength; the ability to bend metal or warp wood by disturbing their molecules; and, perhaps the most useful of all, teleportation, that is, the ability to travel great distances in seconds by simply visualizing the destination.

Of you choose this power, write 'Thaumaturgy' on your *Action Chart*.

An advanced form of Enchantment, Telergy is the power of mind control, telepathy and auto-suggestion. It enhances the tangibility of the illusions of Enchantment and allows you to control the minds of others. However, like Enchantment, some magical beings will be able to resist this power.

If you choose this power, write 'Telergy' on your *Action Chart*.

Where Elementalism allows a wizard to summon the aid of the elemental spirits, the higher magick of physiurgy grants the wizard mastery over the elements. It allows him to command winds, open cracks in the earth, cause earthquakes, raise storms and create other weather effects.

If you choose this power, write 'Physiurgy' on your *Action Chart*.

## Theurgy

Theurgy is an advanced form of Alchemy. Possession of the Moonstone of the Shianti makes the casting of a larger number of spells possible. It unlocks the knowledge of more ingredients for mixing potions and reveals some of the special times, or ways, that they must be mixed. The power of the Moonstone acts as a charm for these potions. No WILLPOWER points are required to make use of the power of Theurgy but you are dependent on discovering the necessary ingredients for your potions during the course of your adventure.

If you choose this power, write 'Theurgy' on your *Action Chart*.

## Visionary

With the aid of the Moonstone, you may use the skill of a Visionary to look upon events that are taking place elsewhere. The power of a visionary is generally concerned with visual images of the present.

If you choose this power, write 'Visionary' on your *Action Chart*.

## necromancy

Necromancy is a higher form of Evocation. Where Evocation allows contact with the spirit world, Necromancy allows a wizard to command the dead, though this is forbidden by Shianti law. It also allows him to make an incantation that will imbue the Moonstone with a protective aura of light to keep away all creatures of evil, dead or alive.

If you choose this power, write 'Necromancy' on your *Action Chart*.

# Wizard's Staff.

Your Staff is your most valuable possession. It looks and feels like an ordinary quarterstaff, yet it is stronger than any known metal. This is your only combat weapon, for you are untrained in the use of any other form of armed combat. It contains a potent force that is unleashed at will by the power of your mind, and causes a beam of destructive power to hurtle from its tip. Every time you unleash this power you must deduct 1 WILLPOWER point.

In the event that your enemy survives such an attack or should you fall victim to a surprise attack, you will be forced to engage in close combat and must attempt to strike your enemy with the Staff. If your attack is successful, a bolt of energy will be released from the Staff that is capable of inflicting great physical harm. If you wish to increase the amount of damage that you inflict in this way, you must use more WILLPOWER points and multiply the number of ENDURANCE points lost by the enemy accordingly. For example, if you choose to expend 3 WILLPOWER points on your attack, all enemy ENDURANCE point losses would be multiplied by three.

If you enter combat with your Staff, deduct 6 points from your COMBAT SKILL. If you have no weapon at all, you must deduct 8 points from your COMBAT SKILL.

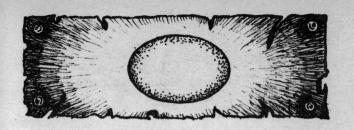

The Moonstone has many attributes, some of which
are described in the higher magicks section and some
of which you will discover during the course of your
adventure. The Shianti have also given it the power
to teleport you to Shasarak *once* during the course of
your adventure. You will be told of that opportunity
when the time is right.

## EQUIPMENT

You wear the grey robe and hooded cloak of a
Shianti Wizard. Your only weapon is your Wizard's
Staff (note this on your *Action Chart* under
Weapons). You wear a Backpack containing 4 Meals
(note under Meals on your *Action Chart*), and you
have been given a map of the Shadakine Empire
(note under Special Items on your *Action Chart*),
which you place inside your robe.

If you have chosen Alchemy as one of your Magical
Powers, then you will have a leather pouch for herbs
and potions hanging from your belt. The Herb Pouch
contains the following:

2 empty vials for carrying potions
1 vial containing saltpetre
1 vial containing sulphur

Your Herb Pouch will carry a maximum of eight items.

## How to carry equipment

Now that you have your equipment, the following list shows you how it is carried. You do not need to make notes but you can refer back to this list in the course of your adventure.

WIZARD'S STAFF – carried in the hand.
BACKPACK – slung over the shoulder.
MEALS – carried in the Backpack.
THE MOONSTONE – carried in the hand or in the Backpack, you must decide which. If carried in your Backpack, note it on your *Action Chart*. It counts as 1 item.

Any weapons and Special Items that you possess as a result of completing previous Grey Star adventures should be entered on the *Action Chart* at the beginning of this book.

## How much can you carry?

*Weapons*
The maximum number of weapons that you may carry is *two*. Your Wizard's Staff counts as one weapon.

## Backpack Items

These must be stored in your Backpack. Because space is limited, you may only keep a maximum of eight articles, including Meals, in your Backpack at any one time.

## Special Items

Special Items are not carried in the Backpack. When you discover a Special Item, you will be told how to carry it.

## Nobles (Shadakine currency)

These are carried in the pocket of your robe.

## Food

Food is carried in your Backpack. Each Meal counts as one item.

Any item that may be of use and can be picked up on your adventure and entered on your *Action Chart* is given capital letters in the text. Unless you are told it is a Special Item, carry it in your Backpack.

## How to use your equipment

### Weapons

Your COMBAT SKILL depends on your Wizard's Staff. If you do not possess your Staff when you enter combat you must deduct 6 points from your COMBAT SKILL. If you enter a combat without a weapon,

31

deduct 8 points from your COMBAT SKILL and fight with your bare hands. If you find a weapon during the adventure, you may pick it up and use it. (Remember that you can only carry *two* weapons at once.)

## Backpack Items

During your travels you will discover various useful items which you may wish to keep. (Remember that you can only carry a maximum of eight items in your Backpack at any one time.) You may exchange or discard them at any point when you are not involved in combat.

## Special Items

Each Special Item has a particular purpose or effect. You may be told this when the item is discovered, or it may be revealed to you as the adventure progresses.

## Currency

The currency of the Shadakine Empire is the Noble, which is a small jade stone. The system of money is alien to the Shianti and for this reason you begin your adventure with no money. Whenever you kill an enemy, you may take any Nobles belonging to him and keep them in the pocket of your robe.

## Food

You will need to eat regularly during your adventure. If you do not have any food when you are instructed to eat a Meal, you will lose 3 ENDURANCE points.

# RULES FOR COMBAT

There will be occasions during your adventure when you must fight an enemy. The enemy's COMBAT SKILL and ENDURANCE points are given in the text. Grey Star's aim during the combat is to kill the enemy by reducing his ENDURANCE points to zero, while at the same time losing as few ENDURANCE points as possible himself.

At the start of a combat, enter Grey Star's ENDURANCE and WILLPOWER points and the enemy's ENDURANCE points in the appropriate boxes on the Combat Record section of your *Action Chart*.

The sequence for combat is as follows:

1. Calculate your current COMBAT SKILL total, based on the weapon you are using. (Remember, if you enter combat without your Staff, you must deduct 6 points from your COMBAT SKILL. If you have no weapon at all, you must deduct 8 points.)

2. Subtract the COMBAT SKILL of your enemy from this total. The result is your *Combat Ratio*. Enter it on the *Action Chart*.

3. If you are using your Wizard's Staff, decide how many WILLPOWER points you wish to use. (Remember, you must expend at least 1 point.) Enter this number on your Combat Record in the box marked WILLPOWER

**Example**

Grey Star (COMBAT SKILL 15, WILLPOWER 23) is ambushed by a Deathgaunt (COMBAT SKILL 20). He is not given the opportunity to evade combat, but he can use his Wizard's Staff against the creature as it swoops down on him. He subtracts the Deathgaunt's COMBAT SKILL from his own, giving a *Combat Ratio* of −5. (15 − 20 = −5). −5 is noted on the *Action Chart* as the *Combat Ratio*. Grey Star decides to use 2 WILLPOWER points, which is noted on the WILLPOWER box of the Combat Record.

4. When you have decided upon the number of WILLPOWER points you wish to use, and you have your *Combat Ratio*, pick a number from the *Random Number Table*.

5. Turn to the *Combat Results Table* on the inside back cover of the book. Along the top of the chart are shown the *Combat Ratio* numbers. Find the number that is the same as your *Combat Ratio* and cross-reference it with the random number that you have picked. (The random numbers appear on the side of the chart.) You now have the number of ENDURANCE points lost by Grey Star. To calculate the number lost by the enemy, multiply this by the number of WILLPOWER points that Grey Star elected to use. Now you have the final number of ENDURANCE points lost by both Grey Star and his enemy in this round of combat. (*E* represents points lost by the enemy; *GS* represents points lost by Grey Star.)

## Example

The *Combat Ratio* between Grey Star and the Deathgaunt has been established as −5, and Grey Star's WILLPOWER points used as 2. If the number taken from the *Random Number Table* is a 6, then the result of the first round of combat is:

Grey Star loses 4 ENDURANCE points.
Deathgaunt loses 5 ENDURANCE points, multiplied by 2 WILLPOWER points, giving a total of 10 ENDURANCE points lost in all.

6. On the *Action Chart*, mark the changes in ENDURANCE points to the participants in the combat, and Grey Star's amended WILLPOWER points total.

7. Unless otherwise instructed, or unless you have an option to evade, the next round of combat now starts.

8. Repeat the sequence from stage 3.

This process of combat continues until the ENDURANCE points of either the enemy or Grey Star are reduced to zero, at which point the one with the zero score is declared dead. If Grey Star is dead, the adventure is over. If the enemy is dead, Grey Star proceeds but with his ENDURANCE and WILLPOWER points reduced.

**A summary of Combat Rules appears on the page after the *Random Number Table*.**

## Evasion of combat

During your adventure you may be given the chance to evade combat. If you have already engaged in a round of combat and decide to evade, calculate the combat for that round in the usual manner. All points lost by the enemy as a result of that round are ignored, and you make your escape. Only Grey Star may lose ENDURANCE points during that round, but then that is the risk of running away! You may only evade if the text of the particular section allows you to do so.

# SAGE ADVICE

Now begins the last and most dangerous stage of your quest to vanquish the Wytch-king, Shasarak. Beware, for you must face many dangers before you are able to confront him at last.

You will find items that might be of assistance on your quest. Some Special Items will help you, others may be of no use at all. You must decide what to keep.

Special care must be taken when selecting your Magical Powers. Make sure that your combination of higher and lesser magicks covers every eventuality. Also, it is worth remembering that some of these Magical Powers will be of little use to you during this part of your quest: choose the powers you think you are most likely to require at this stage.

Be cautious in your use of WILLPOWER points, as your WILLPOWER is the energy source for both your Magical Powers and your Wizard's Staff. If you have a low WILLPOWER score when you confrton Shasarak, you may be easily defeated.

Follow the path of wisdom, Wizard Grey Star. The way of fools is the road to destruction!

At last you hold the fabled Moonstone in your hand. It pulses and glows with a strange milky light. Tanith's eyes shine wildly, and your heart pounds with excitement. the Moonstone; ancient vessel of all Shianti wisdom. What secrets, what powers, does this magical artefact hold in its glowing heart? The stone exudes a comforting warmth as it nestles in the palm of your hand and you feel a presence in your mind. You hear a familiar voice and your heart lifts to ever greater heights, for it is Acarya, High Wizard of the Shianti, speaking to you.

'Hail Wizard, son of man. You have succeeded. We, the Shianti, rejoice and praise you. That which you hold in your hand contains the power that will enable you to defeat the evil Wytch-king, Shasarak.

A crowd of excited voices fills your mind as each of the Shianti sends words of congratulations and admiration. The last of these voices is Maiteya, your old friend, the Shianti master who taught you all you know. 'And so, "little one",' he says, affectionately 'now you possess the Moonstone, Shasarak's bane. While you hold it, we, the Shianti, are able to speak with you but this communication cannot be maintained much longer. Because you have the Moonstone, we have sufficient power to return you to the world, but there is much you should know before we do so. Listen well, Grey Star, for I know not when we will speak again.

I. At last you hold the fabled Moonstone in your hand

'Though it seems to you but a short time since you arrived at the Daziarn, seven years have passed here in the material world. During your search for the Shadow Gate, you visited the city of Karnali. Your arrival there inspired a revolution, led by Sado of the Long Knife and his Army of the Freedom Guild. After your departure, the Freedom Guild withstood a great siege by Shadakine warriors, who eventually withdrew defeated, much to Shasarak's displeasure. Word spread of this victory and the strength of the Army of the Freedom Guild grew. Strategically, Karnali was too isolated to make a great impact against the Shadakine Empire, but, due to the surrounding Gurlu Marshes, it remained self sufficient. Soon, many were travelling to Karnali to escape the tyranny of Shasarak's rule. Pockets of resistance broke out in the townships of Wenat, Zhanis, Sena and the city of Forlu, and the Freedom Guild soon dominated the hills and the plains of the south. They raided Shadakine supply trains and succeeded in depriving the empire of much of its wealth, cutting off all land routes to the Port of Suhn, the wealthiest and most important trade centre of the empire. An army is now formed in Karnali and, in three days, it will march against the Shadakine Empire, hoping to take Port Suhn in the first of many conquests. But, unknown to Sado and the Army of the Freedom Guild, a vast Shadakine force has been mustered in the Sadi desert. Soon, it will march against them. The Army of the Freedom Guild number ten thousand to the Shadakine's thirty thousand. The Freedom Guild cannot hope to succeed against such overwhelming odds. You must save them. Take then to the Forest of Fernmost. It is most important that you go there. There is little time and much to do Grey Star . . .'

The voice grows faint and you realize that the Shianti will be unable to maintain contact for much longer.

'And now, Grey Star, the contact breaks and we must return you to the world to begin the last of your great labours. Are there any last words of advice we can offer you?'

Your mind races as you think of all that you might need to know.

If you wish to know where the Shianti intend sending you, and where in the Shadakine Empire your quest will begin, turn to **348**.

If you wish to hear the Shianti's own advice, turn to **6**.

If you wish to see Shasarak himself, and perhaps discover something of his plans, turn to **340**.

### 2

Alas, you have been too much weakened by earlier struggles. His strength has mastered yours as the last of your own life force is drained from your body. You have lost the duel and doomed all humanity to endure the reign of Shasarak's evil cruelty.

You have failed, your adventure is over.

### 3

You and Tanith each grab a handle and begin to turn them. The wheels creak as the rope coils slowly around one end of the mounting. Pick a number from the *Random Number Table*.

If the number you have picked is 5–9, turn to **63**.

If the number you have picked is 0–4, turn to **79**.

## 4

You walk over to the Phinomel plant and examine it closely. It is flowering well and should provide a large supply. Gingerly you reach forward. The secret is to reach behind the pods and twist their stalks with a swift, nimble movement: it will require a cool, steady hand.

Add together your current WILLPOWER and ENDURANCE totals. Pick a number from the *Random Number Table* and add it to the result.

If your total is *50* or more, turn to **11**.
If your total is *30–49* turn to **16**.
If your total is less than *30*, turn to **40**.

## 5

You triumph and, with a last surge of energy, throw Shasarak tumbling to the end of the hall. Unfortunately the force of the attack shatters your Staff. On hands and knees, Shasarak crawls towards the wall of fire, muttering in choked breaths, 'You shall not have me. You shall not have me.'

Suddenly he reaches out with his hands. 'Agarash, our bargain!' he screams. Agarash laughs once more. A plume of flame snakes out from the wall and wreathes itself around the Wytch-king.

If you wish to allow Shasarak to step through the flaming wall, turn to **350**.
If you possess 3 WILLPOWER points, and wish to fill the Moonstone with your power and hurl it against the wall, turn to **316**.

## 6

'We will advise you as best we can,' he replies. 'Although it is your own wisdom that has brought you, this far, you should not be afraid to trust your own judgement. In the matter of the inevitable challenge of Shasarak, we advise you not to stand against him immediately. He embarks now on a war that will be costly to his strength and demanding of his powers. Wait for him to weaken himself with some great deed of sorcery before journeying into his dark halls for the final duel. First ensure the safety of the Army of the Freedom Guild. Without your help, they will perish. Be on the constant lookout for allies, for the Wytch-king has many enemies, and look to the Forest of Fernmost – a mighty power dwells there and it will do well in your service.'

His voice grows faint.

Turn to **326**.

## 7

At the expense of 2 WILLPOWER points, you summon the mighty powers of the waters of the river Dosar, bending the river to your need. Suddenly a tall tower of water explodes all around the bridge, breaking its stones and instantly destroying the once sturdy structure.

Turn to **75**.

## 8

It looks likely that you will have to do battle with the demon horde. You decide to take advantage of the protection the Theurgic Potion offers and quickly swallow the dark, bitter liquid. Gradually your body begins to glow with a strange, blue light. Remember that the effects of the Potion will begin to fade in only a few hours.

Delete the Potion of Invulnerability from your *Action Chart*. You may keep the empty vial and include it as an item on your *Action Chart*: keep it in your Herb Pouch *or* in your Backpack.

Turn to **121**.

**9**

'Wait here,' you instruct Tanith.

'Wait?' she retorts, defiantly. 'Have I not stood by you in the face of terror, fought at your side, matched you, courage for courage, deed for deed?' She sniffs derisively. 'I'll not stand back now like some feeble girl afraid of her own shadow!'

You know there is no point in arguing with her, especially when so much of what she says is true. The two of you stride forward, prepared to meet whatever danger awaits you together.

You have travelled for two miles when Tanith stops, peering into the shimmering heat haze and shielding her eyes against the sun with her hand. 'They come,' she says, dispassionately.

Following the direction of her gaze, you see something stirring in the distance. You notice a low dust haze hanging in the air, a running cloud drifting against the flat expanse of the plain. There are four runners and they are heading straight towards you. As they come closer, you are able to see that they are ghastly, malformed creatures, each deformed in a different way. These are demons, summoned long ago by the Wytch-king, Shasarak, to plague the tribe of the Masbaté, the warrior people that ruled here before Shasarak unleashed the demonic horde that destroyed them. When the demons had fulfilled their purpose, Shasarak left them to roam these plains at will, instead of returning them to the deep hell from which he summoned them. The leading creature has green, shining skin and a tail. Its neckless head bears the features of a toad. With a feral scream it charges towards you. The others follow.

If you wish to attempt a long-range attack with your Wizard's Staff, turn to **69**.

If you wish to wait for them to approach, so that you can engage them in close combat, turn to **187**.

If you have the Magical Power of Sorcery, and wish to use it to aid you in the battle, turn to **196**.

If you have the Magical Power of Thaumaturgy and wish to use this higher magick to aid you, turn to **203**.

If you have the Magical Power of Enchantment and wish to use it, turn to **211**.

If you have versed in the higher magick of Telergy, and wish to use it, turn to **217**.

## 10

It is the morning of the day you must attempt to close the demon portal of Tilos. You bid Tanith a sad farewell. Eyes brimming with tears, you share a fond embrace before she is led east along the mountain trail by a Masbaté warrior, towards whatever doom awaits her at the hands of Mother Magri in the city of Suhn. She can be saved only by a swift and total victory over the Wytch-king.

You turn to King Samu. 'We must prepare to move,' you say. 'Gather your men. We must make plans.'

If you are versed in the higher magick of Theurgey, turn to **15**.

If you are versed in the higher magick of Thaumaturgy, turn to **19**.

If you are versed in the higher magick of Necromancy, turn to **24**.

If you do not possess any of these powers, or do not wish to use them, turn to **29**.

## 11

With consummate ease, you manage to strip the plant of its pods entirely. Your harvest yields nine pods. They are so small that nine pods only take up the space of three items in your Herb Pouch. Remember to write the Phinomel pods on your *Action Chart*. If there is not room in your Herb Pouch, you may carry some, or all, of the Phinomel pods as Backpack Items.

With a satisfied nod, you finish packing away your new find and continue on your journey.

Turn to **43**.

## 12

You smash the fabric that binds the skeleton's body but you are fighting the creature with magic. Your fellow soldiers do not have the same advantage and the air is filled with their terrified cries. Many are being slain and, as they die, Shasarak's spell takes them, and they rise to fight once more as soldiers of the undead. Those that survive find themselves fighting their friends and comrades. The powers you possess protect only you from attack. You can save the Freedom guild only by destroying Shasarak. The time has come: you must go to him.

If you are versed in the higher magick of Thaumaturgy, deduct 2 WILLPOWER points from your total to cast a teleportation spell, and turn to **39**.

If you have a Temeris potion, you may use it to teleport without using any WILLPOWER points; turn to **39**.

If you are using the power of the Dimension door locked in the Moonstone, deduct 4 WILLPOWER points from your total to teleport, and turn to **39**.

If you are unable to teleport by any of these means, then you have failed in your quest and your adventure is over.

**13**

The creature falls dead amid a flurry of fiery blows. As you fought, the rest of the pack have been creeping towards you slowly and now stand only a few yards away. The death of their leader caused great consternation among their ranks, although they seem confident enough to attack at any moment. They realize now that you fight alone.

If you wish to fire a long-range blast from your Staff, before turning and running, turn to **22**.

If you wish to turn and run immediately, turn to **27**.
If you wish to stand against the demon horde, turn to **54**.

## 14

You turn east. The sun's heat grows less intense as the day passes and you are able to walk at a quicker pace. The afternoon passes and, though there are still several hours of daylight left, your anxiety grows. There has been no sign of a stream or water hole and you will never find one in the dark. You will be able to survive for some time without food but you must find water soon.

Tanith looks around uneasily. 'We are being watched,' she says. You nod. You can also feel the weight of many eyes bearing down on you. Malevolence hangs heavily in the air.

If you are carrying the Moonstone in your hand, turn to **81**.
If you are carrying it in your Backpack, turn to **213**.

## 15

In the Lissan Plain the herbs and flowers that you need to mix a potion of invulnerability grow in abundance. Made from the leaves of the Zakutsk flower and the root of the Demeril bush, the potion is mixed with salt and spring water beneath the rays of the mid-day sun. It will protect your body from physical harm for only a few hours, but might prove invaluable in your attempt to close the portal of Tilos should you be forced to face an attack by the demons of the Lissan Plain, either on your way to the portal, or afterwards, when you are trying to lure the demon horde against the Shadakine army marching towards the birdge at Lanzi.

If you wish to ask the Masbaté to gather the in-gredients for the potion, turn to **34**.

If you prefer to use the higher magick of Thaumaturgy, turn to **19**.

If you prefer to use the higher magick of Necromancy, turn to **24**.

If you prefer not to use the Magical Powers of Theurgy, Thaumaturgy, or Necromancy, turn to **29**.

## 16

Careful as you might be, you are unable to avoid disturbing a Phinomel branch to your left. Two pods emit a jet of viscid purple fluid. One jet misses but, unfortunately, the second splashes your arm, quickly burning through the fabric of your robe and causing a searing pain as it burns your flesh. You lose 2 ENDURANCE points. You have managed to procure six Phinomel pods. As they are so small, the six pods take the room of only two items in your Herb Pouch. If there is not room in your Herb Pouch, you may carry some, or all, of the pods as Backpack Items.

Despite a rather painful experience, you nod to your-self approvingly, sure that the Phinomel pods will be useful, and continue on your search for Lake Dolani.

Turn to **43**.

## 17

With a scream, the horseman falls dead. Quickly you run over to his body. By stealing the dead horseman's uniform, you will be able to lead the demon horde against the Shadakine Army more easily, for the Shadakine will think that you are one of their own.

If you still have your Simar stallion, turn to **285**.
If the stallion has been killed, turn to **292**.

## 18

Without the cognitive powers of Prophecy or Psychomancy, it is impossible for you to locate the mechanism that will open the doors. The only other solution is to use force but, judging from the thickness of the stone doors, it is likely to require a great deal of strength to break them open.

If you have the Magical Power of Thaumaturgy, and wish to use it to open the doors, turn to **295**.

If you have the Magical Power of Sorcery, and wish to use it to force open the doors, turn to **255**.

If you have the Magical Power of Elementalism, and wish to summon an elemental to open the doors, turn to **289**.

If you have learnt the higher magick of Physiurgy, and wish to use it, turn to **181**.

If you wish to resume your journey towards Lake Dolani or do not possess these powers, turn to **234**.

## 19

By using the Magical Power of Thaumaturgy, you will be able to weave a spell of invulnerability about yourself. The cost of this spell will be 4 WILLPOWER points if you wish the effect to last several hours.

> If you wish to create this spell of magical protection about yourself, to help you in your bid to close the demon portal in the hills of Tilos, delete 4 WILLPOWER points from your WILLPOWER score and turn to **57**.
>
> If you wish to use the higher magick of Necromancy in your bid to close the demon portal, turn to **24**.
>
> If you do not wish to use either of these powers, or do not possess them, turn to **29**.

## 20

Stunned and dizzy, you lie on the floor, unable to defend yourself. The Demon Master hovers above, its leathery wings beating. It stoops to deliver a killing blow. Bravely Tanith steps forward, dagger in hand, ready to defend you to the last. The demon minions swarm forward in glee and the position looks hopeless. Then, amid the whirl of your thoughts, you hear the cries of men and the clash of steel. Joyfully you see a gleam of shining metal flash above your head and the Demon Master's back arch with pain. Howling in agony it begins to fall. With lightning reactions, Tanith drags you to one side, seconds before the life-less and bloody corpse of the beast hits the ground with a jarring crash. A long, slim javelin protrudes from its back.

'Grey Star,' Tanith cries. 'We are saved!'

She helps you into an upright position and you peer down the hall. Pouring through the entrance of the tomb comes a mass of tall warriors, swords bared and reaping a deadly harvest among the demonic ranks.

Turn to **38**.

## 21

At the cost of 1 WILLPOWER point you raise the Moonstone and light begins to pour from it. Shasarak scowls and takes a step back.

'So you think the Moonstone is enough to defeat me do you? You forget the need for a mighty hand to wield it. Are you mighty, Grey Star?'

Shasarak's words strike you like blows but you do not fail in your resolve. Effortlessly, Shasarak drains 1 WILLPOWER point and 1 ENDURANCE point from your body. You stagger as the life force is dragged from you.

'You see?' Shasarak sneers.

If you wish to shield yourself with the Moonstone's light, turn to **92**.

If you wish to strike Shasarak with the Moonstone's light, turn to **190**.

## 22

At the cost of 2 WILLPOWER points, you fire into the demon ranks. Two fall dead instantly and the rest scatter with howling shrieks and bestial cries. You turn and run, Tanith at your side. Your attack has bought you time to try to escape the overwhelming number of demons.

Turn to **89**.

## 23 – *Illustration II (overleaf)*

Bathed in the radiant aura of the Moonstone's protection, you continue the journey east. You top a rise and look down its gentle slope. Ahead, you can see a

II.  Four fearsome creatures mount the rise

sparkling river. With a cry of joy, you and Tanith run towards it. At the water's edge you both drop to your knees to drink. Scooping up great mouthfuls of the cool water, you quench your raging thirst. You are on the banks of the Dolani river. Tanith tells you that its source is to the north east, in the Kashima Mountains. Its southerly course leads to lake Dolani, which she guesses to be at least thirty miles away. The river is too wide and deep to be crossed here, although it is likely to be narrower and shallower further upstream. At this point the light of the Moonstone, which you laid on the ground beside you before beginning to drink, starts to flicker as the power of your incantation fades. Suddenly Tanith cries out.

'Grey Star!' she screams. 'We are attacked!'

You snatch up the Moonstone and spin round. Four fearsome creatures have mounted the rise behind you. As you watch, they rush towards you, coming to a cowering halt within twenty paces of you both. Afraid of the fading aura of the Moonstone as the light decreases, each takes another shambling step towards you. They are ghastly, malformed creatures, each with a different misshapen form. These are demons summoned long ago by the Wytch-king Shasarak to conquer the people who once inhabited the Lissan Plain. Having fulfilled their purpose, they were left to roam the plain by Shasarak. The leading demon – the largest – takes another step forward, its glistening green skin and toad-like features reflected in the dull light of the setting sun.

If you wish to continue the necromantic incantation of protection that has almost faded from the Moonstone, turn to **35**.

*(continued over)*

If you prefer to launch long-range attack at the leading demon with your Wizard's Staff, turn to **65**.

If you wish to wait to see what the demons will do, turn to **93**.

## 24

By using the Magical Power of Necromancy, you will be able to create an aura of protection against the forces of evil. You will have to expend 3 WILLPOWER points to light the Moonstone.

If you wish to use 3 WILLPOWER points to create an aura of protection, turn to **57**.

If you are versed in the higher magick of Thaumaturgy, and prefer to use this power, turn to **19**.

If you do not wish to use either of these powers, or do not possess them, turn to **29**.

## 25

You both drink long and deep: the large bowl is almost empty before your thirst is sated. When you have finished you walk to the far end of the hall. Two flights of stairs lead up to a large platform. At the rear of the platform a vast and elaborate frieze has been carved from the wall. In the centre, a woman stands with arms outstretched in a gesture of welcome. She is wreathed in light and, standing all around her, are rows of men and women of proud bearing. This building must be the work of the Masbaté. The woman is a representation of the Great goddess Ishir, High Priestess of the Moon, mother of all men, and the building is some form of temple or shrine.

Another flight of steps leads from the platform to one of the many galleries that line the temple's walls. Cautiously you both mount these steps, passing through a doorway that opens on to one of the galleries. The fading light from above does not illuminate the high archways that lead off the gallery, and, at the cost of 1 WILLPOWER point, you cause a light to glow from the top of your Staff. You peer through an archway to see a large chamber, its high ceiling lost in shadow, its corners shrouded in cobwebs. In the middle of the chamber stands a long pallet of grime-encrusted marble. With a start, you realize that a human form rests upon the pallet, but your panic soon subsides, for it is a dead man, a giant, with a huge broadsword clutched to his chest with withered hands. A necklace of blue stones hangs around his neck; a circlet of silver crowns his head. The brown, shrunken flesh has been partly preserved by some process of mummification, but the garments the corpse wears have all but mouldered away.

Inspection of the remaining chambers on this floor confirms that this is an ancient Masbaté tomb. Each chamber is a crypt, in which the Masbaté have laid their dead to rest with their weapons of war and personal effects. The tomb of the Masbaté was probably served by guardians before Shasarak summoned the plague of demons that eventually destroyed the Masbaté tribe. Tanith arms herself with a long dagger from one of the chambers. She also takes a sling and a number of stones. You may keep any of the following items that you find in the various chambers:

1 coil of Rope (Backpack Item)

1 Sword and Sheath (hung from the belt)
1 Spear (held in the hand)
1 Dagger and Sheath (hung from the belt)
1 Water Bottle (hung over the shoulder by a strap)
4 unlit Torches (1 Torch counts as 1 Backpack Item)
1 Tinder box (Backpack Item)

Remember to mark any items that you keep on your *Action Chart*.

The light from the shafts has faded completely. Night has fallen. You are both very tired and, after further exploration, you discover an empty chamber and both settle down to sleep.

Turn to **200**.

# 26

You focus your will on the stone fabric of the bridge, using 2 WILLPOWER points. With a thunderous explosion, it collapses into rubble and falls into the waters below.

Turn to **75**.

# 27

Instantly you make a dash in the opposite direction. With a murderous howl, the pack chases after you. They are hot on your heels, and within moments you are caught and dragged to the ground.

You have failed in your quest and your adventure ends here.

## 28

The demon opens its mouth and bares a tangle of fanged teeth. It lunges at you, and, as you swerve to receive its attack, you realize that your back is undefended against the other three demons. However, you must fight the toad demon first.

Toad Demon: COMBAT SKILL 17    ENDURANCE 16

You may only evade combat if you have lost less ENDURANCE points than your enemy in the first round of combat.

If you evade combat turn to **41**.
If you win the combat within three rounds, turn to **72**.
If you and the enemy are still alive after three rounds of combat, turn to **87**.

## 29

'You will need to be able to move fast to escape the demon horde,' says Samu. 'Long ago, we of the Masbaté bred a strain of horse called the Simar, renowned for its stamina and the ease with which it can be controlled. It will not shy away from danger.'

A great white stallion is brought before you, harnessed and saddled. Gratefully, you thank Samu for his gift. The Masbaté are summoned and stand fitted and accoutred for battle before their king in a rocky escarpment shaped like a vast amphitheatre. They number a thousand men: a small number perhaps, but a mighty army nevertheless, for the Masbaté are formidable warriors. In a rousing speech, Samu tells them of the battle to come at the bridge at Lanzi, where you will rid their homeland of the demon plague forever. You receive a great cheer before Samu leads his people out of the mountains, towards Lanzi. A guide leads you to the other side of the mountains. The Shadakine Army is expected to reach the bridge at Lanzi within a day. In that time you must close the demon portal in the hills south of Tilos and lead the demons through the forested pass and against the Shadakine Army.

At last you come to the edge of the Lissan Plain and your guide prepares to leave. Before he goes, he offers you the following items to help you in your adventure. You may keep any or all of them.

1 Backpack
1 Coil of Rope (Backpack Item)
1 Water Bottle (Special Item–slung over the shoulder by a leather strap)
1 Tinderbox (Backpack Item)
1 Sword (Weapon)
1 Masbaté Battle Horn (Special Item–hung over the shoulder by a strap)

The guide returns to the mountains. You are alone. You urge the Simar horse into a trot and head north.

If you are already using the high magick of Necromancy in the form of an incantation, turn to **70**.
If not, turn to **76**.

## 30

With the Moonstone and your Staff held aloft you shout down at the demon horde, 'Begone creatures of darkness, minions of hell, slaves of terror! Beware the might of the Shianti and the sacred Moonstone of old.'

Many of the smaller demons begin to whimper obscenely, while others vanish, blinking out like candles snuffed by the wind. You step on to the next stair and note with satisfaction that they hasten away with anguished cries, endeavouring to remain outside the protective ring of the Moonstone. Just as you begin to think that your ploy will work, a large shadow looms at the far end of the hall. A winged form stands silhouetted by the sunlight streaming through the entrance to the tomb. The sea of deformity parts before you and the timid moans and cries become crowing gloats of pleasure. To your dismay, the protective light of the Moonstone gutters as the power of your incantation begins to fade.

Turn **270**.

## 31

You rein the exhausted stallion to a halt. Your whole body aches as a result of its relentless, galloping stride. You gaze westward, certain that the pack are in pursuit, but there is no sign of them. Time passes and you begin to feel uneasy. The plain is flat and featureless, and the afternoon sky is clear enough to be able to see far into the distance, yet there is no sign of the demon plague.

If you wish to backtrack a little, turn to **51**.
If you wish to continue east, turn to **47**.

## 32

With a low rumble, the stone door opens slowly, the

rusted metal of the pulleys screeching amid the rasp of grating stone. The door is only half-way open when it grinds to a halt. The age-old mechanism has failed. However, the gap is sufficiently wide to admit a human form and soon you and Tanith are standing within the ziggurat, peering anxiously into the shadows.

Turn to **135**.

### 33

The horseman's blow shears his pear in half as he gallops past. He wheels, sword drawn, and dashes towards you again. Now you must fight to the death.

Shadakine: COMBAT SKILL 19    ENDURANCE 16

If you win the combat, turn to **17**.

### 34

After many hours, the ingredients are brought to you. they must be ground and mixed together, then heated over a fire to form the potion. You wil need a pestle and mortar and at least one empty vial to do this. A Masbaté medicine man offers you the following to help you make the potion:

> 2 empty Vials for carrying potions
> 1 Vial containing saltpetre
> 1 Vial containing sulphur
> 1 Pestle and Mortar
> 1 Tinderbox

Remember to mark any items that you take on your *Action Chart*. The empty vials, and those containing sulphur and saltpetre can be stored in your Herb

Pouch. You may also keep a sprig of Zakutsk flower and a Demeril root, these must be carried in your Herb Pouch. The Pestle and Mortar are Backpack Items and the vials may be stored in your Backpack *or* your Herb Pouch.

Turn to **49**.

### 35

At the expense of 2 WILLPOWER points, the Moonstone begins to glow brightly and, as you repeat the words of your necromantic incantation, the radiant whiteness of its aura increases, clothing you and Tanith with luminescence. The toad demon gibbers, slavers, and then retreats with its arms thrown up in front of its disfigured face. The other demons howl in tortured anguish and back away. They linger outside the protective ring of the Moonstone, pacing in front of you, spitting and snarling their frustration.

If you wish to attack at long range with your Wizard's Staff, turn to **46**.
If you wish to advance on the demons and attempt to engage them in combat, turn to **105**.

### 36

As the evening draws in, the temperature begins to cool. You are tired and thirsty. You have been heading in the direction of Lake Dolani but neither you nor Tanith have ever been to the Lissan Plain before and you are not sure of the lake's exact location. You know only that it lies on the southern side of the plain. You are now unsure that you can reach it by nightfall. Looking to the west, you see a large building of square, tiered stone. It is approximately two miles away.

If you wish to investigate the building, turn to **297**.
If you prefer to continue, turn to **234**.

## 37

Entranced, the rider trots towards you, hailing you as friend, for your magic controls him completely. When he has come close enough, you grab his leg and drag him from the saddle. So sudden is your action that the warrior is unable to resist. A swift blow to the back of his head knocks him unconscious. Now you can complete your plan. By dressing in the Shadakine uniform, you will be able to lead the demon host towards the Shadakine Army and they will think you one of their number. Quickly you don the uniform. Your Simar steed is exhausted but the Shadakine horse offers the chance of a fresh mount and greater speed. You slap the Simar's haunches and watch it trot away. The beast has served you well, and you offer a silent Shianti blessing that will keep it from harm.

Turn to **250**.

## 38

Your vision clears and, as you regain your senses, you see that the warriors are men of the Masbaté, the tribe believed to be extinct after persecutuion by the Wytch-king, Shasarak. With a flurry of sword blows, the Masbaté hew a bloody path towards you. Though they number less than fifty, their demonic foes seem powerless to resist, so swift and fierce is the attack.

The demon horde scatters in all directions. Some demateril ize – magic is inherent in their nature. Those that remain are slain mercilessly.

When at last the battle is done, no living demon remains in the tomb, while, incredibly, the Masbaté have suffered no losses, only a scattering of light wounds. One of their number now stands before you. Like his comrades, the Masbaté warrior stands well over seven feet tall, his body rippling with muscle beneath skin as black as ebony. His hair is long and black and his eyes still burn with the fire of battle. He is clad only in a corselet of worn, padded leather. A scabbard slung low from a broad belt carries a massive broadsword of dull, grey metal. His only protective wear, a pair of metal wristbands, is engraved with the intricately worked design of a rearing horse. He gives you a speculative stare. It is not an altogether friendly gaze.

'What do we have here?' he booms, in a strong, yet melodious bass tone. 'A boy and a girl perhaps? Or demons in human guise, defilers of the sacred tomb of our forefathers. Speak now and swiftly. My blade is thirsty yet to drink the blood of more hellspawn.'

Before you are able to speak, Tanith has risen to her feet, brandishing her dagger and scowling with the characteristic ferocity that you have come to know so well. 'You know not what you say,' she snaps, menace in her voice. 'But for that, this blade of mine would have your life for such insult to one who comes to save your brawny, worthless hide. Soften your tone, tall one, for you speak to a mighty wizard, a master of great powers, the chosen one of the great ancient Shianti. He has come to challenge the Wytch-king himself, who is surely the enemy of us all.'

Despite her slight frame and her puny blade, Tanith confronts the warrior with an icy countenance that would freeze blood. Though he towers over her like a giant, the warrior steps back, mouth agape in astonishment at her fearless outburst. He is stunned into silence. The barely suppressed mirth of the other Masbaté is plain to see.

'Ho there Dioka!' shouts a squat Masbaté, with a bellowing laugh that makes his pot-belly quiver and shake. 'It's a spitting she-cat that's stolen your tongue I see.'

'And the cat has claws, bladder belly!' she snaps. The plump warrior's face drops, while the one named Dioka bursts into laughter. 'Well met, my lady,' he guffaws.

With a bemused expression, you rise on shaky feet and turn to Dioka. 'Greetings, men of the Masbaté,' you call out in a loud voice, ensuring that all can hear. 'Plainly we are not agents of evil in mortal guise.'

'Indeed not,' Dioka replies with a smile. 'The very demons of the plain would flee the wrath of your brave companion's acid tongue!'

'Yet, in her anger she spoke the truth,' you continue. 'For I am the Wizard, Grey Star, bound upon a quest in the service of the Shianti and sworn to the destruction of the Wytch-king, Shasarak.' The vast hall grows silent. Wide-eyed, the Masbaté regard you with stunned expressions.

'Can this be?' Dioka gasps, a gleam of hope shining in

his dark, deep eyes. 'We will talk of this at length and in the proper place,' he continues. 'You must come with us. It is not wise to remain here. The demons may return and in greater numbers. Most likely they will be led by more formidable masters than this,' he gestures dismissively towards the corpse of the Demon master that sprawls on the floor a few feet away. The home of the Masbaté now lies in the Kashima Mountains, beyond the River Iss. The king must hear of your return.'

The Masbaté restore the bodies of their ancient dead to their resting places. A funeral pyre for the slain demons is built outside the walls of the tomb, and with considerable effort and over many hours, they are able to repair the stone door. While they work, your wounds are attended to and you and Tanith are given food and water. There is a gifted healer among them and he is able to restore to you 1 ENDURANCE point. (Amend your *Action Chart* accordingly.) It is late afternoon before the Masbaté are ready to leave. Struggling to keep pace with the rapid march of the warriors, you head into the lengthening shadows, toward the distant mountains: the secret lair of the last of a proud and mightly race.

Turn to **260**.

### 39 – *Illustration III (overleaf)*

Suddenly you are in a wide, round hall, full of shadows. At one end of the hall is a flaming wall, and kneeling before the wall is the hunched figure of Shasarak, Wytch-king of Shadaki. His back is turned to you but he spins round the instant you arrive. He is a hideous sight. His flesh is black as if burnt by recent

III. Shasarak's stare burns into you with intense hatred

fires and his fingers are like claws. Half his face is missing, and in its place there is a metal plate, which is the only thing that gives shape to a livid mass of shrunken flesh and tissue. One eye is shrivelled, sightless and shrunken, the other burns into you with hatred so intense that it almost forces you back a step.

The room fills with the sound of savage laughter, but it is not Shasarak who laughs. A familiar, slithering, deathly voice emanates from the wall of fire, and within the fire you see two slanted eyes: pools of absolute darkness. It is the Demon Lord, Agarash!

'See, Shasarak. He has come, as I told you he would. He has come to slay you. Won't you accept my bargain?'

'NEVER!' Shasarak hisses, his voice like the rush of broken stone scattering on the floor. 'He does not have the power to master me . . . as you have not, Demon.'

Shasarak glares at you malevolently and raises a damaged hand. He is about to strike.

If you wish to raise the Moonstone against Shasarak, turn to **21**.

If you wish to defend yourself with the Moonstone, turn to **92**.

## 40

Though you handle the branches of the plant delicately, you cannot avoid disturbing it and many of the pods squirt jets of purple fluid. Fortunately, many miss you. Two of the jets, however, splash your arm. The acid eats quickly through the fabric of your robe and burns into your flesh. You lose 3 ENDURANCE points. You have managed to take three Phinomel pods. Because they are so small the three pods count as only one item in your Herb Pouch. If there is not room in your Herb Pouch, you may carry the pods in your Backpack.

Cursing your own clumsiness, you pack away your new find, certain that the pods will prove useful, and resume your search for Lake Dolani.

Turn to **43**.

### 41

With the speed of a pouncing tiger, you twist around to face the three that remain. They are almost upon you, but the speed of your reactions and the fierceness of your gaze paralyses the grotesque creatures. With a mighty cry, you hurl yourself at them in a wild blaze of magical fire and slashing blows. At the cost of 1 WILLPOWER point, your Staff crashes down on the head of the nearest demon. It falls to the ground with a squeal of pain, smoke curling around its purple body that shines like the shell of a giant beetle. It reaches at you with a feeble motion, its crab-like pincer flexing stiffly before it dies. Those that remain flee as fast as their distorted limbs can carry them, wailing in a frenzy of insane fear. You start to pursue, but before you can reach them they have dematerialized. You turn around: the injured toad demon has also disappeared. Panting heavily, you satisfy yourself that Tanith is unharmed before dropping your guard. You fall to your knees, drawing great breaths and leaning heavily on your Staff.

Turn to **201**.

**42**

Other dots appear high on the horizon. Approaching at an alarming speed are a multitude of strange and sinister ceatures. You count twenty at least. A familiar sound greets your ears: the babbling frenzy of the demon horde close behind you. There is no time to prepare magical spells, nor is there anywhere to hide, and the forest pass must be at least twenty miles away. You feel sure you can outrun the demon horde – but the flying creatures? You have only two choices.

> If you wish to attempt a last, desperate dash for the pass, keeping clear of the flying creatures as best you can, turn to **202**.
>
> If you wish to make a stand against the flying creatures, in the hope of despatching them before the demon horde reaches you, turn to **223**.

**43**

You come to the top of a small rise. Peering over the edge, you see that the ground slopes away in a long, shallow curve, which rises on every side to form a broad basin. At the centre lies a large lake many miles wide. Feverishly you lick your lips in anticipation of a long, languorous drink of cool water. You start to move down the slope when Tanith catches your arm.

'Wait!' she says. 'I can see something down there.'

You follow the line of her finger. Among the verdant grassland of the depression that surrrounds what must be Lake Dolani you can just make out a human form. You edge a few more feet down the slope. With horror you see a large man lying with his arms and legs tied to four wooden stakes driven into the ground. A faint moan drifts on the breeze: he is calling for water. You edge a little closer. The man is almost a giant, measuring at least seven feet tall. His skin is black as ebony and his hair is long and flowing. Suddenly you realize that this is one of the Masbaté, the original inhabitants of the Lissan Plain and a mighty warrior people – till Shasarak defeated them in the Plains War of MS 5008.

You have only known one Masbaté: Samu, a noble and fearless warrior, who accompanied you in your search for the Moonstone. Once, he was king of the Masbaté nomads. He thought himself the only survivor of his people – it was common belief that the Wytch-king had hounded the tribe into extinction, sealing their doom by unleashing a plague of demons. Some say that these demons roam the plains still.

You wonder who has left the poor, tortured man to die in the sun. You step further down the slope intending to free him, but Tanith holds you back, fearing a trap. You cannot see how anyone, even Shasarak himself, could know that you have returned to the lands of the Shadakine empire after an absence of seven years.

If you have the Magical Power of Prophecy, and wish to use it, turn to **58**.

If you are versed in the higher magick of a Visionary, and wish to use this power, turn to **67**.

If you do not possess either of these powers, or do not wish to use them, turn to **85**.

**44**

The hatred and the fear are too much for your soul to

bear. Your mind lacks the strength to withstand the horror of the demon horde. The light of the Moonstone dwindles and, with the fading of its light, the demon horde swarms out of the valley of fear. You are dragged from your steed and delivered as an offering to the unknown power that dwells on the other side of the portal. It drinks your soul with a hideous cackle of triumph.

You have failed. Your quest ends here.

## 45

Spellbound, the rider heads towards you. As he draws alongside, you drag him from his saddle. A swift blow to the back of his head renders him unconscious. Quickly you don his uniform. By dressing in the Shadakine uniform you wili be able to lead the demon host towards the Shadakine Army without being attacked, for they will think that you are one of their own.

Turn to **250**.

## 46

You take aim at the nearest of the demons, the smallest of the four. Its back is bent and its arms end in crab-like pincers. Its purple body shines like the shell of a giant beetle. You release a bolt of magical fire that rips through it and hurls it to the ground, squealing with rage and pain, before it lapses into lifeless silence. You have expended 2 WILLPOWER points. The remaining three demons step back in alarm, cowering.

If you wish to charge at the remaining three, turn to **105**.

If you wish to fire a long-range attack at another demon, turn to **117**.

### 47

The miles roll by and eventually, the Simar steed adopts a more relaxed pace. You estimate that you are half-way to the pass. Looking over your shoulder to the west, you see only the broad expanse of the plain and the distant hills of Tilos. Of the demon plague you can see nothing.

High in the afternoon sky you see two black specks wheeling above you. As you walk, one of them begins to spiral downwards. It is a long, snake-like creature with broad, feathery wings. Its talons are like small, clutching needles and it has a small set of forelimbs. The other creature follows and, to your surprise, you see that it is exactly the same as the first, only smaller. That these are plague demons is certain, but it is the first time you have ever seen two of the same kind. The Flying Snakes make no move towards you; they merely drift on the air currents. Evidently these are not affected by the Agarash's inspired state of crazed frenzy.

If you wish to attack one of the Flying Snakes with your Staff at long range and you have 2 WILLPOWER points, turn to **88**.

If you wish to ignore them, turn to **103**.

### 48

Close examination of the well reveals that the rope is rotten and likely to snap if you use the handles to draw up the receptacle attached to it. You decide, therefore, to haul up the rope by hand. You do this, drawing up a large, clay bowl, full of clear water.

Turn to **25**.

## 49

The potion is mixed under the sun's rays and the light you have summoned from the Moonstone. You must fill one of your empty vials with the fluid that is produced. (Delete one of your empty vials from your *Action Chart*.) You have now created a Potion of Invulnerability. Mark this as a Special Item, which may be stored in your Backpack or your Herb Pouch.

Turn to **57**.

## 50

A swirl of colour passes before your eyes. Intinctively you reach for Tanith's hand and clasp it tightly. The walls of the circular chamber shimmer in and out of focus: the Shianti are transporting you from the Daziarn plane to the real world. A brilliant flash of light fills the room and you close your eyes involuntarily. When you next open them you look upon a vast plain of grass that undulates like the sea beneath a clear, sunlit sky. The journey is complete.

The Moonstone is still in your hand. However, where once it shone with the purity of white light, it now glows a smoky grey. You can but guess at the meaning of this transformation.

If you have the Magical Power of Prophecy, and wish to use it, turn to **162**.

If you do not have this power, or do not wish to use it, turn to **239**.

## 51

You lead the Simar steed slowly to allow him some rest. Stopping and shielding your eyes from the sun, you gaze into the distance. Suddenly something clutches at your feet and tries to drag you down. A small, green-skinned demon like a hairless ape has crawled through the knee-high grass. You have walked into a trap. More ape demons leap out of the grass around you, their eyes blazing with unreasoning hatred and you attempt to fend off the nearest of your foes who, even now, clutches at your legs. You cannot evade this combat. The demon is only three feet tall making it harder to hit him: deduct 1 from your COMBAT SKILL for the duration of the fight.

Ape Demon: COMBAT SKILL 20    ENDURANCE 15

If you win the combat in three rounds or less, turn to **109**.

If you win the combat in four or more rounds, turn to **123**.

## 52

You skirt the edge of the valley, keeping a great distance between yourself and the hell below. You feel the burning heat of countless eyes concentrated on you. At last you reach the other end of the valley. You lift the Moonstone high in the air and point it at the gate. A hiss floats up from the valley. You allow the protective aura to fade and begin to concentrate your mind upon the Moonstone and the closing of the portal. The host creeps towards you. They seem to sense that the power of the Moonstone is now being diverted.

If you wish to expend 2 WILLPOWER points in a long-range attack at the demons below with your Wizard's Staff, turn to **73**.

If you do not wish to attack them turn to **78**.

### 53

Taking Tanith by the hand, you stride forward. The demons retreat before you, gibbering with fear and cowering in the Moonstone's light. You come to the top of the stairs that lead into the hall.

Turn to **30**.

### 54

It is a brave but foolish decision. How could you hope to stand against so many? After a valiant defence, in which many demons are slain, you are killed by the evil horde.

Your life and your quest end here.

### 55

Your heart is pounding as you teleport through the stone door. A sickening feeling is followed by absolute blackness, chill and silent. Then you appear on the other side: you have succeeded. The use of this spell has cost you 2 WILLPOWER points. Looking up, you see a long, thick rope trailing from an opening in the side of one of the doors. You reach out and pull.

Turn to **32**.

## 56

A moving cloud in the sky attracts your attention as you stand panting over the last of the fallen beasts. It is a flock of Winged Demons, and they are heading straight towards you. At your back, the yammering horde draws ever closer.

You sprint away again, travelling as fast as you can.

Turn to **309**.

## 57

When the spell is cast and the protection complete, you turn and face Samu. 'I am ready,' you say. 'Summon your men, we must make ready to leave.' 'I have a gift for you, Grey Star,' he replies.

Turn to **29**.

## 58

Using your power, you probe into the near future. You sense that there is danger nearby: the Masbaté is being used as bait for a trap, and the danger lies in venturing into the basin. The use of this Magical Power has cost you 1 WILLPOWER point.

If you still wish to go to the aid of the Masbaté, turn to **97**.

If you prefer to leave the man to suffer, and hide behind the ridge that overlooks the lake, turn to **116**.

If you are versed in the higher magick of a Visionary, and wish to use it to discover more before you make your choice, turn to **67**.

## 59

You maintain your rapid pace and sit up in the saddle. The Flying Snake alters the course of its flight with precision and dives towards you at lightning speed. As it swoops over you, it rakes your shoulder with a sharp talon before climbing back into the sky. Both the snake and the horse were travelling so fast that there was no time to use your Staff in self defence. Your shoulder starts to bleed: lose 1 ENDURANCE point.

Turn to **42**.

## 60

You set a brisk pace for more than an hour but then the burning sun slows you down. Tanith, too, looks very weary. Your throat is parched. Neither you nor Tanith have seen a waterhole or anything that could yield nourishment or moisture and there has been no sign of any living creature. You are further disturbed by the sight of a lone figure heading towards you from the south. It is too distant for you to be able to distinguish any details, but it is moving at great speed. You peer into the shimmering heat and try to guess what it is that approaches.

If you wish to stand your ground and wait for the figure to arrive, turn to **267**.
If you wish to advance against it, turn to **273**.
If you wish to try to evade it, turn to **286**.

## 61 – *Illustration IV (overleaf)*

With a dry swallow, you urge the white stallion down the slope and into the valley. You can feel its mighty

IV.  You look upon a valley of fear crawling with the demon host

heart thumping against its ribs, matching the speed of your own. With the Moonstone held high above your head you move through the ranks of the Demon host. Gibbering with fear, they shield their eyes from its pure, white light and back away, stumbling over one another. The sea of deformity parts like a tall swathe of grass to let you pass. Resolutely you stare ahead ignoring the hideous mass of malignancy that surrounds you; nothing must distract your gaze as you focus on the flaming archway that draws nearer with each tentative step of the stallion's hooves. Now, the moment of no return, of death or triumph, has come. You release your necromantic aura of protection and begin anew, focusing your mind on the Moonstone and on the closing of the portal. The demon horde wavers, but only for a moment: they are still spellbound by your presence and intimidated by the Moonstone.

Turn to **112**.

## 62

Looking up, you see the forest some five hundred paces away. You put on a last desperate spurt in an attempt to reach the safety of the woods. Your body is racked with pain and exhaustion, your lungs feel as if they are on fire and your heart pounds relentlessly. You stumble. You are not sure if you have enough strength to succeed.

Pick a number from the *Random Number Table*. Add this number to your current ENDURANCE total.

If the total is 12 or more, turn to **71**.
If the total is less than 12, turn to **96**.

## 63

The rope is attached to a large, clay bowl, brim-full of clear water. You secure the handles so that the bowl does not drop to the bottom of the well. The well must stand over the site of an underground spring, for the water is fresh.

Turn to **25**.

## 64

You take aim once more and send a bolt of magical flame rushing towards the Flying Snake. Once more your aim is true and the creature drops dead with a shrill cry of pain. The attack has cost you 2 WILLPOWER points.

Turn to **240**.

## 65

You raise your Staff and unleash a magical beam of fire at the toad demon, using 2 WILLPOWER points. It howls with pain and staggers back. Thick, black blood oozes from the wound you have inflicted in its side but it is not slain. It cowers before you, staring with malevolent hatred, pure evil visible in its small, red-veined eyes. With a tormented scream it vanishes and the remaining three advance on you. Suddenly Tanith's warning alerts you to something standing close behind you. You spin round, poised to strike, your staff held firmly in both hands and your body crouched in a combat stance, to see the injured demon leering down at you. It has barely completed its magical materialization when it moves to strike.

Turn to **28**.

## 66

You are just about to unleash the power of your Staff when the Flying Snake abruptly changes direction, manoeuvring into a dive. It hurtles towards you at lightning speed, inflicting a raking claw wound on your shoulder as it passes, before climbing into the air. Both the Flying Snake and the horse were travelling so fast that you were unable to retaliate. You have lost 1 ENDURANCE point.

Turn to **42**.

## 67 – *Illustration V (overleaf)*

Taking the Moonstone in both hands, you gaze into it and concentrate with all your power. The stone is transformed into a whirlpool of spinning colours. Then, abruptly, it clears and you are looking upon Lake Dolani. Nearby lies the Masbaté, still bound and suffering. You struggle to extend the range of the image in the stone. and eventually your efforts are rewarded. A swarm of creatures comes into view. Moving along the base of a line of mountains is a monstrous horde of deformity: the demon plague. Each of the creatures has a different but equally misshapen form: wierd toadbeasts, their green hides glistening, crawl and flop along the ground; stumbling apes with stunted limbs shamble beside creeping reptiles with human heads. You are sure the demon plague is very near and you sweep the land once more, tracing the line of a river that fills a lake similar to Lake Dolani: this must be Lake Iss. Another group comes into view. It is a band of Masbaté warriors, moving swiftly along the line of the river and most certainly headed towards their fellow warrior

V. Taking the Moonstone in both hands you concentrate on it
with all your power

and the trap laid by the demon horde. Your concentration begins to ebb. You can no longer maintain control of the Moonstone and you allow the image to fade. The use of this power has cost you 2 WILLPOWER points.

If you wish to go to the aid of the captured Masbaté, turn to **97**.

If you prefer to leave the man to suffer and hide behind the ridge that overlooks the lake, turn to **116**.

If you wish to head in the direction of Lake Iss and attempt to warn the Masbaté warriors of the trap that awaits them, turn to **89**.

### 68

The demon clings to the side of the stallion and, with a superhuman effort, you twist round and bring your Staff crashing down on its skull. The creature falls to the plain, spinning over and over again before coming to rest. Your heart lifts as you notice the growing frequency of trees and bushes dotting the land: the forest's edge is rushing towards you. The winged demons above are now unable to fly so low. The demon horde is still far behind. With a jubilant yell you enter the sanctuary of the wooded pass through the mountains and, swiftly, you dismount, wincing at the pain caused by your many cuts and bruises. The stallion is also injured and you lead the exhausted animal along the heart of the forest. Looking around furtively you eventually find a hidden clearing where you can rest for a few moments and plan the last stage of your task.

Turn to **170**.

**69**

You take careful aim and unleash a bolt of destructive power from the tip of your Staff. A beam of incandesence banishes the shadows of the evening and spears the demonic creature before you. The force of the blast knocks the creature off its feet and inflicts a terrible wound in its side that oozes with viscous black blood. The attack has cost you 2 WILLPOWER points. The other creatures come to an abrupt halt, watching in amazement as the injured demon clambers to its feet. It stands at a distance, cowering and snarling. The other three imitate their leader, panic writhing in their ghastly faces.

If you wish to charge them, turn to **232**.

If you wish to make another long-range attack, turn to **243**.

If you wish to stand your ground and await their next move, turn to **262**.

**70**

The pure white light of the Moonstone shines forth with a lambent glow. Bathed in the protective aura of the Moonstone, you ride on with speed. The miles are covered swiftly and the snow-white stallion maintains a tireless, unfaltering pace; you bless Samu for such an invaluable gift. At last you reach the River Dolani. The river is close to its source in the mountains and is consequently quite shallow; you are able to ford it easily. After crossing the river, you veer slightly to the north west, towards the hills that lie south east of Lake Tilos, where the portal of the demons of the Lissan Plain is situated. In the distance, you see a small group of figures heading towards you.

If you wish to avoid this gathering, turn to **224**.
If not, turn to **231**.

### 71

With a last, painful effort you hurtle through the brush and undergrowth at the edge of the forest. Using the cover of the forest you soon leave the horde struggling behind you. Stumbling with fatigue, your robe tattered and torn, your body bleeding from a dozen small wounds, you tramp through the densely packed vegetation. At last you find a hidden glade and you stop to rest for a moment.

Turn to **170**.

### 72

With a wide, scything stroke of your Staff, the demon is slain. Its ruined body crumples to the ground, staining the grass of the plain with thick, black blood. Suddenly a razor-sharp pincer grabs your arm, raking your shoulder to inflict a bloody wound (you lose 3 ENDURANCE points). The other three demons have crept up on you while you fought. Your attacker is the smallest of the three: a grotesque creature with an impossibly bent back and a bulbous purple body, shining like the shell of some gigantic beetle. With a cacophony of triumphal screeches they throw themselves at you. You cannot evade and must fight them to the death. All three fight as one enemy.

Three Demons of the Plain:
COMBAT SKILL 20      ENDURANCE 30

If you win the combat, turn to **251**.

## 73

A cascading arc of fire flows from your Staff to rain death on the valley below. Two demons shriek and are silent; another scurries back and forth screaming as its body burns. Terror spreads through the horde and it advances no further. You have made a wise decision. This demonstration of your power has been sufficient to hold the beasts at bay. Deduct 2 WILLPOWER points for this magical attack.

Turn to **112**.

## 74

At the expense of 2 WILLPOWER points, you throw a beam of fiery magic into the ranks of the demon horde. A ghoulish form with three arms and grey, mottled skin falls dead, followed by a strange, bird-like creature with the body of a worm. You begin to walk down the stairs towards the rest of the horde. Flinching at the Moonstone's light they back away. The power of your incantation is beginning to fade now but you feel sure that the horde is sufficiently frightened to allow you and Tanith to pass. As you reach the bottom of the stairs, you are disturbed to hear their moans of fear change to a gloating croon. They part before you to reveal a giant shadow at the far end of the hall.

Turn to **270**.

## 75

You are given a horse and ride alongside Samu, who, like the rest of the Masbaté, does not ride. The Masbaté are too big to ride and use their Simar horses only to carry their supplies. Nevertheless, the

Masbaté run like the wind and soon the River Dosar is far behind.

When night comes, you make camp. Tomorrow, your southerly journey will take you to the Army of the Freedom Guild.

Turn to **321**.

## 76

The horse maintains a steady, tireless pace and the miles pass by swiftly. Soon you reach the River Dolani. The river is very shallow at this point and you are able to ford it easily. Heading north west you sight a line of demons coming towards you.

If you possess a potion of Invulnerability, and wish to drink it, turn to **84**.
If you do not, turn to **90**.

## 77

You decide to change direction and increase speed. Shortly your limbs feel weary and your feet begin to drag. The heat of the sun is almost unbearable. You look over your shoulder and, to your amazement, the figure has disappeared. You gaze over the featureless grassy plain: where could he be hidden? You are beginning to suffer from heat exhaustion: lose 1 ENDURANCE point. Your present course is taking you far from anywhere you want to go.

If you wish to head in the direction of the fortress city of Shadaki, turn to **14**.
If you wish to head south, towards the lands of the Army of the Freedom Guild, turn to **36**.

### 78

The demons seem loathe to attack but a large, hulking man-shape with wrinkled, elephantine skin summons up the courage to charge towards you. His sudden attack catches you off-guard and you are unable to evade combat.

Man Demon: COMBAT SKILL 20    ENDURANCE 21

If you win the combat, turn to **144**.

### 79

To your dismay, the rope snaps. A distant splash tells you that the receptacle that was attached to the rope has now fallen to the bottom of the well. The rope must have been rotten with age. You will have to find some other method of drawing water. Leading down into the inky depths you see a series of metal rungs cemented into the walls of the well.

If you have the Magical Power of Elementalism, and wish to use it, turn to **124**.

If you are versed in the higher magick of Physiurgy, turn to **185**.

If you prefer to climb down into the well, or do not possess either of these Magical Powers, turn to **229**.

### 80

Frantically you grab at the armour, trying to drag it off, but the rigours of your flight from the demon host have left you too fatigued to resist the current of the water. In a few, awful moments you drown in the waters of the River Dosar.

You have failed in your quest.

## 81

You glance down at the Moonstone. Shocked, you see that it contains an absolute blackness. It is lifeless and still and the comfortable presence it once radiated is gone. The Moonstone is reflecting the evil nature of the environment that surrounds it.

> If you have the Magical Power of Necromancy, and wish to begin an incantation to ward off evil, turn to **146**.
>
> If you have the Magical Power of Prophecy, and wish to use it, turn to **169**.
>
> If you have the Magical Power of a Visionary, and wish to use it, turn to **177**.
>
> If you prefer not to use any magic, turn to **213**.

## 82

Tanith and Kuna rush to stand at your side. She bares a small dagger but he is unarmed. The reptillian demon hurls himself at you with a fearsome scream. You cannot evade combat as this would mean leaving Kuna and Tanith to face the pack alone.

Reptile Demon of the Plains:
COMBAT SKILL 21      ENDURANCE 22

If you win the combat, turn to **163**.

## 83

Now that you know where the mechanism is you are able to reach out to it with the power of your mind. At the cost of 2 WILLPOWER points you are able to trigger the mechanism of the great stone doors.

Turn to **32**.

### 84

Fearing conflict so early in your journey, you drink the bitter potion of Invulnerability. Soon your body begins to glow with a strange blue light: the protection is complete. Remember that the effects of the potion will fade after a few hours. Remove the Potion of Invulnerability from your *Action Chart*, although you may keep the empty vial, which may be stored in your Herb Pouch or in your Backpack.

Turn to **90**.

### 85

You ponder the choices open to you. While you agree with Tanith that it would be safer to take cover behind the ridge, it pains you to see another human suffer.

If you wish to go to the Masbaté's aid, turn to **97**.

If you prefer to leave the man to suffer while you hide behind the ridge that overlooks the lake, turn to **116**.

### 86

Summoning all your strength, you fight against the fast-moving current of the River Dosar, tugging off the armour. You manage to swim to the other side and drag yourself ashore, panting for breath. A short distance away you can see Samu. Hauling yourself to your feet, you stagger over to him.

'Grey Star!' he gasps. 'You succeeded?'

'Call your men. We must retreat. Look!' you cry hoarsely, gesturing across the river. 'I have brought the demon plague. We must flee while they and the Shadakine fight.'

It is as you say. Across the river the demons do awful battle with the Shadakine. Samu springs into action, blowing upon a horn and sounding the retreat. The Masbaté retire. The Shadakine cannot pursue while the whole demon horde is attacking them. Nevertheless you must destroy the bridge to prevent pursuit should the Shadakine, who number in their thousands, defeat the demon plague too soon.

If you have the Magical Power of Elementalism, and wish to use it, turn to **314**.

If you are versed in the higher magick of Physiurgy, and wish to use it, turn to **7**.

If you are versed in the higher magick of Thaumaturgy, and wish to use it, turn to **26**.

## 87

Despite the seriousness of the gaping wound in its side, the loathsome creature continues to resist you. Suddenly you are thrown forward, hurled to the ground in a flurry of kicks and blows. A razor-sharp pincer bites into your shoulder and you lose 3 ENDURANCE points. The other three demons have pounced on you from behind while you fought.

Thankfully, you have managed to retain a grip on your Staff. You must fight the four demons to the death. Due to the surprise of the attack and the disadvantage of having to fight your way back to your feet you must subtract 2 from your COMBAT SKILL for the duration of the combat.

Four Demons of the Plains:
COMBAT SKILL 21    ENDURANCE 34

If you win the combat, turn to **251**.

## 88

You take careful aim as the snake flies overhead and, at the cost of 2 WILLPOWER points, release a beam of magical flame. With a piping cry it falls to the ground. The other Flying Snake swerves and heads east, flying high in the sky ahead of you.

If you wish to fire at the remaining Flying Snake with your Staff at long range, and have 2 WILLPOWER points, turn to **64**.

If you wish to ignore it, turn to **228**.

## 89

With Tanith at your side, you begin to run with all the speed you can muster. You run along the rim of the rise that overlooks Lake Dolani, hoping to reach the river that fills the lake and effect a crossing there. Chancing a brief look over your shoulder, you see the demon horde in pursuit. Looking ahead once more, you sight a band of tall, black-skinned men in the distance, heading towards you. They are Masbaté warriors, come to save their brother bound by the lake. Panting wildly, you look back to see the demon horde closing the distance between you. Their terrible, inhuman cries are now within range of your hearing and it seems probable that the evil horde will reach you before the Masbaté do.

If you wish to stop and turn to attack, turn to **141**.
If you wish to try to reach the Masbaté before the
  demons reach you, turn to **299**.

### 90

You spur your horse into a gallop and hurtle towards
the demons. Already you can make out the details of
their hideous forms: half-men, half-beasts, with evil
eyes and glistening fangs. Soon a gap of only a
hundred paces stands between you. There are ten of
them and they thirst for your blood.

If you wish to charge the demons, turn to **98**.
If you wish to avoid the demons, turn to **106**.
If you wish to attack them at long range with your
  Wizard's Staff, turn to **114**.

### 91

The power of invulnerability is an immense feat,
requiring great effort. You concentrate your will upon
strenghtening the fabric of your body, immersing it in
waves of sorcery. Your body begins to glow with an
eerie blue light. You stand back and look with disdain
on the first of the demons, the toad beast, as it hurls
itself at you. Its initial blow has no effect on you.
Instead the creature howls in pain and clutches at it's
clawed hand, hurt from the impact of your iron flesh.
The remaining demons make similar attempts to
harm you, all with the same result. When all their
efforts have proved futile they begin to back away,
cowering with fear beneath the intensity of your
unflinching gaze. Impressive as this power is, it has
cost you 4 WILLPOWER points. You raise your Staff,
ready to strike at the nearest of the demons, a vile

hunched figure with snapping, crab-like pincers and a shiny, purple body like a huge beetle. However before you can strike, all four vanish. They do not return.

Turn to **99**.

## 92

Your whole body glows with the Moonstone's protection.

'Afraid to fight?' Shasarak mocks. He does not attack for the moment. Instead, he reaches into the air and produces his own Wizard's Staff; it is long and black. He weighs it casually in his hand. 'Shall we duel now, Grey Star? Or will you stand forever within that damnable light, afraid to fight?'

The voice of Agarash booms from the wall of fire at the end of the hall. 'Who is it that is really afraid to fight, Shasarak, tell me that?'

'Be silent, Demon,' Shasarak commands. 'I'll have this young viper yet.'

If you wish to duel with Shasarak, turn to **131**.

If you wish to throw some of the Moonstone's power at Shasarak, and have 1 WILLPOWER point with which to do so, turn to **145**.

## 93

The toad demon comes snarling and slavering at you, its arms outstretched, long-nailed claws flexing to rake at your flesh. Suddenly it leaps. You step to one side and slam your Staff into its torso, inflicting a dark, oozing wound. It howls in pain and turns clumsily.

You lift your Staff to strike the creature once more as it faces you with small, red eyes that stare malevolently. You swing your Staff but you strike nothing. The demon has vanished leaving only the echo of its tormented scream and the stench of its acrid breath. The three remaining demons advance slowly towards you, gibbering with obscene delight. Using the momentum of your swinging stroke at the toad demon, you spin round to face the three hideous creatures in one fluid movement. They falter, then step back in fear, clinging to each other and shrieking. Suddenly Tanith shouts a warning. There is something close behind you. You turn, Staff upraised, muscles tensed, ready to spring at the injured demon that has magically materialzed behind you.

Turn to **28**.

### 94

You are completely surrounded. There is no escape. Despite your high degree of skill in combat you cannot hope to win against such overwhelming odds. The demons swarm over you like ants, killing you mercilessly.

You have failed in your quest.

### 95

With this change of direction, you increase your pace, but the burning heat drags at your every step and soon you are soaked with perspiration. You stop to draw breath; you look over your shoulder to discover that the lone figure is nowhere in sight. Yet there is no tree, rock or bush anywhere to hide behind. You are suffering from heat exhaustion and must lose 2 ENDURANCE points. Your current course is taking you away from anywhere you want to be.

If you wish to head east, in the direction of the city of Shadaki, turn to **14**.

If you wish to go south, towards the Army of the Freedom Guild, turn to **36**.

### 96

Your body is numb with exhaustion. You stumble once again . . . and fall. With wild gleeful cries, the pack reaches you before you are able to rise. Your last moments are spent regarding the multitude of crazed, hideous faces that crave only your death.

Your life and your quest end here.

### 97

You tell Tanith that you have decided to help the Masbaté and start down the slope. Reluctantly she follows. You reach the man and begin untying the ropes that bind his wrists and ankles. He mutters his thanks in a faint voice and, with your help, he half-crawls, half-stumbles towards the lake, where he begins to drink thirstily. You and Tanith do the same, quenching your day-old thirst with relish.

The Masbaté's name is Kuna. He tells you that he was captured while fishing alone on the banks of the Dolani River, by a number of the demons that still roam the Lissan Plain. He has lain bound since that time.

'The hellspawn knew that my Masbaté brothers would come for me and hoped to trap them in the narrow confines of this enclosed region. But tell me, who are you? Why are you here?' he asks.

Before you can reply, Tanith shouts a warning. Her face is horror-stricken. You turn around, barely able to suppress a shocked gasp at what you see. A ring of grisly beasts lines the curving slope before you in a wide semi-circle. 'This is the demon plague,' you whisper.

The steady croon of hellish voices grows as the evil horde gloats at the utter hopelessness of your position. You are enclosed by a force that numbers almost a hundred. With a terrible cry, a pack of demons rushes towards you. Each of the creatures has a different but equally misshapen form. Some are like strange toad beasts, others are malformed apes with stunted limbs and a shambling gait. The leader of the pack is a large, slimy reptile with a tortured human face. Only moments remain before the pack of demons is upon you.

> If you wish to fire, with your Wizard's Staff at the leader of the pack in a long-range attack, turn to **288**.
> If you wish to stand and receive the charge, turn to **82**.

## 98

With a fierce cry you charge, eyes flashing, Staff blazing. The demon pack comes to a startled halt, amazed at the audacity of your move. You close the gap between yourself and the pack in moments . . . and then the charge hits home.

If you have recently drunk a Potion of Invulnerability, or have the protection of Thaumaturgy, turn to **118**.

If not, turn to **128**.

## 99

With a relieved sigh, both you and Tanith turn to resume your journey east. Night has almost fallen. In the faint light, you see a glimmer in the distance. It is a river. You break into a run and do not stop until you have reached the banks of its fast flowing waters. Hurriedly, you scoop handfuls of water into your mouth, and do not stop until your parched throat is soothed and your thirst quenched. With a satisfied expression, Tanith sits up on her haunches, wiping her mouth with the back of her hand.

'This is the River Dolani,' she says. 'It leads south, to fill the great Lake Dolani thirty miles downstream. Upstream, to the north east, is its source in the Kashima Mountains.'

To continue your journey east you will have to cross this river. It is too wide and deep to be waded, and the current is too fast for you to be able to swim across. You ponder your next course of action, lost in thought.

Turn to **201**.

## 100

Like his comrades, the Masbaté warrior stands well over seven feet tall. Clad in a corselet of worn, padded leather, his body ripples with taut muscle beneath skin as black as ebony. His hair is long and his eyes still burn with the raging fire of battle. He stares at you curiously. 'Who are you?' he asks.

'Greetings men of the Masbaté,' you reply. 'I am Grey Star, Wizard of the Shianti, bound upon a quest in their service, and sworn to the destruction of the Wytch-king, Shasarak.'

'Can this be?' the warrior gasps, shaking his head in amazement. 'We will talk of this later in a safer place. My name is Dioka, chief of this warrior band. Come with us to the mountain lair of the Masbaté in the Kashima Mountains. The demons may return in greater numbers. The King must hear of your return.'

You agree to his request and soon you are struggling to keep pace with the rapid march of the Masbaté warrior as he heads towards the mountains and the secret lair of the last of a proud and mighty race.

Turn to **260**.

## 101

You urge your steed to one last great effort and head straight for the forest. At the forest's edge the plain is dotted with bushes and trees, making it difficult for the Winged Demons to attack and, with a joyful cry, you enter the sheltered sanctuary of the woods. You dismount and lead the stallion along the curving trail that runs through the heart of the forest. Both you and the beast are exhausted and you search for a place to rest. Finding a concealed glade, you stop for a few moments and plan the next course of action.

Turn to **170**.

## 102

Your indecision has granted the demons time to close in and they are now almost at arm's length: you must ready yourself for close combat. The razor-sharp pincer of a hunched creature with the body of a huge beetle rakes at your shoulder: lose 3 ENDURANCE points.

Turn to **264**.

## 103

You continue at a gentle canter, the afternoon sun beating down on you from a clear sky. Periodically you look over your shoulder but there is still no sign of the demon plague. The Flying Snakes keep pace with you for a while, then abruptly climb high into the sky and disappear from view, heading east.

Turn to **247**.

## 104

You are surrounded by hundreds of creatures. They close in with evil expressions on their ruined faces and a giant, wingless bat slashes out at you with its claws. However, you are able to hold your ground unflinchingly, for you feel nothing. Soon a great crowd of demons are slashing and gouging at you but still you remain unharmed and slowly you beat a path toward the portal. As you progress, the light of invulnerability that once enfolded you begins to fade and you begin to feel some pain at fresh blows. You field a brilliant defence, however, taking full advantage of being mounted. More and more demons back away in fear of this indestructible warrior who wields a Staff of burning death.

You use 2 WILLPOWER points and lose 1 ENDURANCE point in your fight to reach the portal. Now, at last, it is at hand. There is a lull in the fighting. The demon pack forms a large circle around you and stand contemplating another charge. You pray that they do not, for your magical invulnerability has faded. You must act swiftly. You draw out the Moonstone and focus your energy upon it. The demon horde wavers.

Turn to **112**.

### 105

Bravely you stride forward, shouting curses and threats at the foul beasts. They shrink back in horror, unable to endure the touch of the Moonstone's light. Suddenly they break into a run. They do not stop until they reach the slope that slants away from the rise, when they turn to shriek and howl at you in one last act of defiance before simply vanishing. You relax your guard and, when you are sure that they will not return, you release the spell of protection from the Moonstone. Its light fades. You notice that now the demons have gone, the Moonstone has returned to the swirling grey state it possessed when you first arrived on the plain.

Turn to **140**.

### 106

Suddenly you wheel, giving the line of demons a wide birth. They also change direction but the speed of your Simar steed is great and you are able to avoid them easily. Soon they have become nothing more than blurs on the horizon.

For a while the journey continues without further interruption, the steady, rolling gait of your Simar mount eating up the miles. Suddenly you hear the flap of leathery wings beating above your head. You look up to see a large, winged reptile bearing rows of razor-edged teeth flying towards you. It gives a terrible scream that echoes all around the open plain.

If you wish to fire a long-range blast at the creature with your Wizard's Staff, turn to **149**.

If you wish to increase the speed of your Simar steed and head towards the beast to engage it in close combat, turn to **161**.

### 107

Taking Tanith by the hand you pursue the demons, who offer no resistance. All their efforts are concentrated on keeping outside the range of your Staff, which you use to prod any demons that remain too close, herding them like a flock of sheep. Soon, you reach the top of the stairs that lead directly to the hall. You step on to the first stair and nod to yourself in satisfaction as they part in haste before you, scattering in all directions. A grisly corridor of malformed creatures forms before you, leading to the entrance of the tomb. Then, their timid moans and cries change alarmingly to an undulating rhythm of crowing pleasure and sneering gloats, and you see a winged form silhouetted by the sunlight that streams through the tomb's entrance.

Turn to **270**.

### 108

At the cost of 1 WILLPOWER point, you weave a web of

enchantment about yourself, creating the illusion that you are a Shadakine warrior. You stand and reveal yourself to the rider, waving and calling him to you.

Turn to **186**.


## 109

After a rapid flurry of strokes from your Staff you deliver a killing blow. The slain demon's fellow attackers are all around, anxious to strike, and in the corner of your eye you glimpse the demon horde sprinting towards you. The attack of these small ape beasts is probably intended only to delay you. You vault into the saddle and the stallion springs away.

Turn to **147**.


## 110

Standing before you is a squat, malformed creature. Its features are grotesque and distorted; its back is bent at an impossible angle; its limbs twist like a gnarled tree. The eyes stare out of a knuckled face at odd angles above a raw gash of a mouth that snarls and spits as you approach. The creature crouches low and then leaps at you. You raise your Staff in readiness but the attack does not materialize: the creature has disappeared! The creature is nowhere to be seen. You look at Tanith, a question half-formed on your lips.

'Some creature of Shasarak's,' she states coolly. 'Demons rule this land now, though once it was a place of untamed beauty. At his command it has become a realm of fear.'

You wonder if the creature has gone to warn others of its kind, or whether it simply fled in fear. Whatever the answer, one thing is certain: you must keep moving. You still have not located any food or water, and evening is drawing in.

If you wish to go east, turn to **14**.
If you wish to go south, turn to **36**.

## 111

Taking careful aim, you release a searing ball of fire and hurl it at the Flying Snake. The demon falls, screaming. The cost of your attack has been 2 WILLPOWER points. An apish beast drifts forward, then dives.

Winged Demon: COMBAT SKILL 20   ENDURANCE 20

Combat lasts one round only as the demon wings past. If your enemy loses more ENDURANCE points than you, ignore any ENDURANCE points loss you incur in this combat.

If you are still alive, turn to **306**.

## 112

You hold the Moonstone above your head as it fills slowly with power and light. A chorus of inhuman moans ripples across the valley and your horse snorts and paws the ground nervously. The rays from the Moonstone play upon the burning archway, and it suddenly bursts into flames. You have used 1 WILLPOWER point in your attempt to close the portal. Now it seems imbued with a new force: a power strong enough to resist even the might of the Moon-stone of the Shianti. Your Simar steed rears and you are almost thrown. The demon horde are paralysed, cowering and whimpering pathetically. Your heart almost stops when a pair of large eyes appears within the flames of the demon portal.

Turn to **158**.

### 113

Holding the Moonstone above your head you begin the incantation of protection. You notice that the Moonstone is filled with an absolute blackness: it is reflecting the evil presence of the demons. As the spell takes effect, the Moonstone shines forth anew with a white, radiant light that banishes the shadows of the tomb. The use of this magical Power has cost you 2 WILLPOWER points. A babble of discontent breaks out from the creatures below. The light of the Moonstone has revealed your position. A scuffle of webbed and clawed feet tells you that the demon horde is rushing up the stairway towards you. The only way down to the hall is by the stairway and the only exit from the tomb is through the entrance to the hall.

If you wish to release a long range attack at the demon horde with your Wizard's Staff, turn to **174**.

If you wish to head towards them, turn to **215**.

### 114

At the cost of 2 WILLPOWER points, you take careful aim and release a bolt of magical energy at an indistinct figure in the demon line. With an anguished cry it falls to the ground. But still the demons approach relentlessly.

If you wish to charge, turn to **98**.
If you wish to try to evade the demons, turn to **106**.


## 115

Although you have discovered the location of the triggering mechanism, it cannot be activated without using the powers of Sorcery or Thaumaturgy. You will, therefore, have to force open the door. It is very strong and the use of force against it may use up many WILLPOWER points.

If you have the Magical Power of Elementalism, and wish to summon elemental aid, turn to **289**.
If you have learnt the higher magick of Physiurgy and wish to use it, turn to **181**.
If you do not possess these powers, or wish to take up your journey to Lake Dolani once more, turn to **234**.


## 116

You clamber up the slope once more but as you reach the top you see a horde of demonic creatures heading towards you from the west. Quickly you and Tanith duck down below the ridge. The demons will be upon you soon.

If you wish to try to flee the approaching horde, turn to **89**.
If you wish to remain where you are and surprise the horde as it approaches, turn to **126**.

## 117

Taking advantage of the demons' confusion, you release another charge of magical flame, sending it arcing towards the toad demon. This action costs you 2 WILLPOWER points. Thick, black blood drips from the demon's wound but it is not slain. It gives a low growl before it and the other demons vanish. You breathe a sigh of relief: both you and Tanith are unharmed. You release the spell of protection from the Moonstone and its light fades, returning to its grey, rather than black, state.

Turn to **140**.

## 118

Your body glows with an eerie blue light, your Staff blazes with a blinding white incandescence and your heart pounds with the fury of battle as the great white stallion carries you into the screaming fray of the demon line. Many clawed hands reach out to rend and tear your flesh but you remain unharmed. Others reach for the stallion's bridle in an attempt to stop the mad galloping rush of its charge.

If you wish to fight the demons all around you, turn to **193**.

If you wish to continue your charge and attempt to escape the evil clutches of the demon pack, turn to **207**.

## 119

Standing at the top of the stairs, you look down on the mass of monstrous beings. They are stunned by your unexpected attack, and the protective aura of your necromantic spell causes them to cower before

VI.   Some gurgle obscenely – others growl and roar with crazed expressions

you. The light of the Moonstone shines upon them and they attempt to shield their eyes from its bright light.

> If you wish to hold your position and try to intimidate them further, turn to **30**.
>
> If you wish to release another blast of power at long range with your Staff, turn to **74**.
>
> If you wish to charge them, turn to **293**.

### 120

Your call for aid goes unheeded by the element of earth. Either you have made a demand it does not understand or one it cannot fulfil. Whatever the reason, your attempt has failed.

Turn to **275**.

### 121 – *Illustration VI*

They are moving faster now. Some gurgle obscenely, others growl and roar with crazed expressions. It is a grisly host of horrors: twisted faces with bulging eyes; beasts with long, fleshy tentacles or waving insect feelers. A parasitic insect with a hard, chitinous shell hangs on to the back of a tusked reptilian with tiny suckers, draining the reptile of nourishment but providing it with the armoured protection of its own body. All these and hundreds more seek you out, their courage growing by the moment.

> If you wish to ride to the other end of the valley, using the high ridge above the slopes, and attempt to close the portal without combating the demons, turn to **233**.

*(continued over)*

If you wish to charge the demon horde, turn to **218**.

If you wish to attack the demon horde with a long-range burst from your Staff, turn to **204**.

### 122

As you have already located the door mechanism, it is a simple matter for a Thaumaturgist to exert sufficient magical force to trigger it. With a minimum of effort you set into motion the sequence of pulleys and weights behind the door. The use of this spell has cost you only 1 WILLPOWER point.

Turn to **32**.

### 123

No sooner have you slain the demon than three others of its kind launch themselves at you. As you fight, another of the creatures attempts to slay your horse, while in the distance you glimpse the entire demon horde. Even at this distance you can hear their blood-curdling howls. The stallion neighs and rears to attack his assailants with his hooves. You must fight the three ape demons that beset you.

Three Ape Demons:
COMBAT SKILL 24    ENDURANCE 25

If you wish to evade combat after the first round, turn to **155**.

If you do not evade in the first round of combat, you must fight to the death. If you win, turn to **168**.

## 124

You close your eyes and sink into a trance state. Reaching out to the Elemental plane, you summon the aid of the Water Elementals at the cost of 1 WILLPOWER point. After a short pause you hear the sound of rushing water at the bottom of the well. Then, suddenly, a whirling column of water rises out of the well, carrying on its tip a large, clay bowl. You reach out and take the bowl: it is brim-full of water. The waterspout subsides.

Turn to **25**.

## 125

Pain sears your body as the black fire hits you: reduce your ENDURANCE total by half, rounding fractions up to the nearest whole number. All the while the foul laughter of Agarash the Damned fills the hall. At the cost of 1 WILLPOWER point you strike Shasarak's head with a powerful blow. His tortured scream fills the air, and he grabs at your Staff. He will not let go, and a shimmering burst of fire travels from Shasarak's hands up the length of your Staff. Shasarak is using it as a bond between you. He is attempting to pit all his remaining strength against yours.

If you wish to continue this duel of life forces, turn to **310**.

If you wish to evade this combat by wrenching your Staff from Shasarak's hand, turn to **129**.

## 126

With bated breath you wait below the crest of the slope. When you consider that sufficient time has passed you spring to your feet, Staff ablaze, ready to strike. Your timing is perfect. The pack is almost upon you but your sudden appearance brings them to a halt. You wonder if you have taken on too much, for you can see that the pack numbers almost a hundred. They are a monstrous gathering of creatures: sub-human malformations and unnatural mixtures of bestial and human features. Before the pack realizes that you are alone, you charge, falling upon the leading demon, a large, slimy reptile with a twisted human face.

Reptile Demon: COMBAT SKILL 21   ENDURANCE 22

If you win the combat, turn to **13**.

### 127

You change direction and attempt to increase your pace, but the heat is too intense. Soon you are panting for breath and your body is soaked with sweat. After a short time you are forced to stop for rest. You look around but can see no sign of the distant figure. It has disappeared, although there is nothing to hide behind. Your efforts in the fierce sun have cost you 1 ENDURANCE point. You wonder if the sun is having as bad an effect on your mind.

Turn to **14**.

### 128

You thunder into the demon line, riding one of them down in a stampede of dust, blood, and flashing hooves. As you sweep past, another of the demons, a vile, rat-like creature with the body and legs of an ape, grabs at your saddle. It vaults on to the Simar's haunches and clutches at your throat. Deduct 2 points from your COMBAT SKILL for the duration of the struggle as the demon is attacking you from behind. You must remain mounted as the Simar Horse gallops across the plain.

Rat Demon:COMBAT SKILL 19    ENDURANCE 20

If you win the combat, turn to **136**.

### 129

With a mighty effort you drag the Staff from his hand before the life force is drained from you. Shasarak drags himself to his feet and begins to run towards the wall of fire.

'Come, come to me,' Agarash whispers. 'I will be free.'

Shasarak stops. 'No, you will not have me,' he rasps savagely. 'I'll take him yet.' He reaches up and pulls a long, black Staff from thin air and brandishes it at you. 'Come . . . we will fight!' He lashes at you with his Staff. You must duel with your arch enemy.

Wytch-king Shasarak:
COMBAT SKILL 10    ENDURANCE 20

If you win the combat, turn to **180**.

### 130

You teleport but as your body begins to rematerialize you are filled with terror. You have reappeared inside a wall beside the doorway. Your body is racked with a brief but severe pain before you die, half-embedded in a solid wall of granite.

Your life and your quest end here.

### **131** – *Illustration VII*

Without warning you charge while Shasarak crouches in a hunched combat stance.

'It is better this way,' Shasarak snarls, twisting his Staff in his hand.

Wytch-king Shasarak:
COMBAT SKILL 30    ENDURANCE 30

If you win the combat, turn to **180**.

### **132**

With a mental effort that requires 2 WILLPOWER points you float into the air, hovering above the head of the shrieking demons as they reach out at you with flailing limbs. Although you are now safe from their evil clutches, Tanith remains on the ground. A demon reaches for her, a grotesque creature with a hunched back and the body of a huge, purple beetle. She backs away, nimbly avoiding the clutch of its razor-sharp pincers. While there is still a short distance between them you must strike.

If you wish to fire a long-range attack at the beetle demon with your Wizard's Staff, turn to **143**.

If you wish to release your power of levitation and drop down on the creature from above, turn to **248**.

### **133**

You command the Shadakine warrior to ride towards you; the warrior obeys. The use of this spell has cost you 2 WILLPOWER points.

Turn to **186**.

VII.   Shasarak crouches in a hunched combat stance

## 134

The portal is near enough for you to be able to attempt to close it. Unfortunately, when you cast the shining power of the Moonstone on to the burning gate you will reveal yourself to the evil host that lurks in the valley below.

> If you wish to remount your Simar steed before making the attempt, turn to **139**.
>
> If you prefer to make the attempt from your hiding place at the edge of the valley behind the ridge, turn to **153**.

## 135

You are looking into a long, broad hall, dappled with pools of faint orange light. The source of the light is a series of square, slanting shafts high in the tall, vaulted ceiling. At the far end of the hall are two staircases, each leading to the first of many galleries that run along each wall. Archways line the balustraded galleries, each one leading into an ominous pool of darkness.

Your footsteps echo loudly as you walk across the tiled floor covered with the dust of centuries. The air is musty and tainted with the faint aroma of attar. Each stone is draped with cobwebs. You move towards a dais in the centre of the hall. Mounting the steps, you see that it contains a wide, circular opening. A thick, iron bar is suspended across the opening and mounted on each end is a large handle. Attached to the handles and passing through a hole in the middle of the bar is a length of thick rope.

'This must be a well!' exclaims Tanith, excitedly.

If you wish to turn one of the handles and draw from the well, turn to **3**.

If you wish to examine the well, turn to **48**.

### 136

With a backwards jerk, you thrust the butt of your Staff into the creature's ribs. It yammers in pain and falls from the horse: it is dead before it hits the ground. Over your shoulder you see the line of demons recede into the distance. They try to pursue you but the fleet-footed stallion runs as fast as a speeding arrow and the demons soon pass from sight.

Turn to **142**.

### 137 – *Illustration VIII (overleaf)*

Springing to your feet, you hurl a cascading rain of magical fire on to the head of the demonic horde below. Many fall dead and the evil mass is thrown into an uproar of startled shrieks and wails. This magical attack has cost you 2 WILLPOWER points. The scuffles of webbed and clawed feet tell you that a group of demons are rushing for the stairs that lead up to the galleries. The only way to the hall is by those stairs and you can leave the tomb only by the entrance to the hall.

Turn to **236**.

### 138

Your call for aid goes unheeded by the element of water. Either you have made a request that it does not understand or one that it cannot fulfil. Your attempt has failed.

Turn to **275**.

VIII.    You hurl a cascading rain of magical fire on to the head of
the demonic horde below

## 139

Sitting astride the beautiful white stallion, you trot to the edge of the valley overlooking the flaming archway of the portal and draw out the Moonstone. You focus all the power of your will on to the stone and the closing of the portal. A chorus of inhuman moans ripples across the valley. You hold the Moonstone above your head as slowly it fills with power and light. The demons draw nearer and your horse paws the ground and stamps nervously.

Suddenly the flaming archway ignites. Its fire swirls and writhes with great intensity, spitting gouts of liquid orange flame in all directions. You have used 1 WILLPOWER point in your attempt to close the portal but now it seems imbued with a new force, a power strong enough to resist even the ancient might of the Moonstone of the Shianti. Your Simar steed rears up on its hind legs and you are almost thrown. The horde stop as if paralysed, cowering and gibbering pitifully. Your heart misses a beat as a huge pair of monstrous eyes appears within the flames of the portal.

Turn to **158**.

## 140

Night falls over the silent Plain of Lissan and the waters of the river are black and mysterious. Although relieved that your ordeal against the foul demons is over, you are apprehensive at the horrors that a night in this forsaken country might bring.

Turn to **201**.

## 141

Abruptly you turn to face the oncoming horde of malformed beasts. The leading demon, a large, reptilian beast with a twisted human face, lets out a chilling scream.

If you wish to unleash a long-range attack with your Wizard's Staff, turn to **221**.

If you wish to stand and receive the charge, turn to **160**.

## 142

The sun is high in the sky: it is past noon. At last a range of hills comes into view: the hills of Tilos. You have suffered no further attacks nor have you sighted any other demons in the last two hours. Where can they be? Samu said they numbered in the high hundreds. Why have they not sought to prevent you from reaching the hills of Tilos, home of the portal that is the sole gateway to their world?

If you are versed in the higher magick of a Visionary, and wish to expend 2 WILLPOWER points using it, turn to **249**.

If you have the Magical Power of Prophecy, and wish to use it at the cost of 1 WILLPOWER point, turn to **266**.

If you do not possess either of these powers, lack sufficient WILLPOWER points to use them or do not wish to use them, turn to **279**.

## 143

You take aim and release a ball of magical fire that rains down on the hellish creature before it can strike. With an anguished wail it falls to the ground, a great smoking wound in its side. The magical attack has cost you 2 WILLPOWER points. The demons that remain cringe beneath you now. You raise your Staff and prepare to strike again but, before you can do so, the demons vanish, dematerializing in the space of a heartbeat.

Gradually you lower yourself to the ground. Unfortunately you release the power too soon and fall to the ground in a tumble of arms and legs. Tanith giggles. You clamber to your feet with a shrug. 'Well, it's the first time I've ever levitated,' you say, dusting off your robe and blushing scarlet.

Turn to **99**.

## 144

The man demon falls dead and his body rolls back down the slope and into the pack of demons below. They begin to back away. Your display of power is enough to hold the fearful beasts at bay for the moment.

Turn to **112**.

## 145

You hurl a ball of white, glowing power at Shasarak. He flinches and falters. The voice of Agarash cackles. 'Beware the bauble the Shianti holds,' it cries between gulps of perverse laughter. 'It bites! Fight on little wizards, fight on. Such sport you provide. Who could ask for more?'

Turn to **320**.

## 146

Holding the Moonstone aloft you begin an incantation of protection that should discourage any evil creature from attacking. The Moonstone flares and is transformed into a white radiance. The use of this Magical Power has cost you 2 WILLPOWER points. You continue and make good progress as the shadows lengthen.

Turn to **23**.

## 147 – *Illustration IX*

You thunder across the plain at great speed, stopping only to check that the demons are still in pursuit. After an hour of this relentless pace, you estimate that you are half-way to the pass: only forty miles until you reach the cover of the forest. Looking up, you see a small, black speck, high in the air. As it grows closer, you see that it is a large, winged serpent with broad, feathered wings. It has sharp talons and small, clutching forelimbs.

If you wish to attack the Flying Snake at long range with your Wizard's Staff, turn to **66**.

If you wish to wait to see what the beast does, turn to **59**.

## 148

You have never attempted teleportation before. Be careful not to teleport yourself into a stone wall or tree. If you do make this mistake your body will not be able to function and you will die instantly. It is safest to teleport to a place you have seen or already visited so that you can visualize it accurately in your mind. In cases like this, where you have not seen the

IX.   It is a large, winged serpent with broad feathered wings

place you are teleporting to, you must try to imagine your arrival point.

Closing your eyes, you prepare to travel. Pick a number from the *Random Number Table*. If you have the silver charm of Jnana the Wise, add 1 to this number. If you possess the Magic Talisman of the Shianti, add another 1 to this number. You may also add 1 for each of the following Magical Powers that you possess: Sorcery, Prophecy, Psychomancy, Visionary, and Telergy.

If your total is 5 or less, turn to **130**.
If your total is more than 5 turn to **55**.

## 149

The winged reptile is still some way off and the rolling gait of the stallion makes aiming a little difficult. You raise your Staff and release a bolt of power at the beast.

Pick a number from the *Random Number Table*. If you possess the Silver Charm of Jnana the Wise, add 1 to this number. If you have the Magic Talisman of the Shianti, add another 1 to this number.

If your total is now 5, or less turn to **171**.
If you total is now 6 or more, turn to **182**.

## 150

A dazzling whirl of deadly strokes from your Staff fells the grisly creature at last. All around you hear the sound of battle as the brave Masbaté challenge the malevolent fury of the demon horde. The warriors are superb fighters and the demon ranks are soon thrown into disarray. Some of the demons dematerialize by magical means. Those that do not are swiftly slain by the fierce Masbaté.

At last the battle is over: no demons remain alive. To your amazement, the Masbaté have suffered no casualties, though they number only fifty men. Sheathing his long broadsword, one of their number walks towards you. Far off in the distance, you see that the Masbaté man who lay tethered by the lake has been released and a few of his brother warriors are helping him up the slope.

Turn to **100**.

### 151

Quickly you look around. In the crypt where you and Tanith spent the night there is an alcove within the far wall. It is large enough to hold both of you and its shadows are dark enough to keep you from sight.

If you wish to hide in the alcove, turn to **166**.
If you wish to search for a hiding place elsewhere in the gallery, turn to **253**.

### 152

A large Flying Snake hurtles towards you. You hold up your Staff and brace yourself to receive the attack. The beast's razor-sharp talons flex and unflex as it reaches out to grab you.

Flying Snake: COMBAT SKILL 20    ENDURANCE 23

Combat lasts for only one round as the demon speeds past. If your enemy loses more ENDURANCE points than you, ignore the ENDURANCE points you lose.

If you are still alive, turn to **306**.

### 153

Drawing out the Moonstone, you focus all the power of your will on to it and concentrate on the demon portal. A moan ripples through the ranks in the valley below, turning into a chorus of fierce, inhuman cries. Suddenly the portal erupts into an intense blaze of swirling, writhing flame. A large pair of eyes appears in the flames of the portal and a deathly voice speaks. Your Simar steed whinnies in fear, rears up, its hooves flashing in the sun and then bolts, hurtling at high speed away from you. The demon horde sweeps up the side of the shallow valley in their hundreds and attacks. Without your horse, you have no hope of evading them and, after a long, valiant fight in which many demons fall, you are dragged to the ground and slain.

Your quest ends here.

### 154

With a fierce battle cry, you rush forward and, at the cost of 1 WILLPOWER point, you deal a death blow to the nearest demon, a hairless, ape-like creature with a tough red hide. An uproar of shrieks and wails breaks out among the ranks of the beasts, and they rush away from you in fear. Some vanish into thin air, giving a hint of their dark, magical natures.

Turn to **107**.

### 155

Swiftly you twist away from your attackers and vault into the saddle in one fluid movement. The stallion springs into action and the gap soon widens between you and the demon horde.

Turn to **147**.

### 156

You and Tanith climb over the debris of shattered rock and enter the ziggurat. Anxiously you peer through the dust that is still settling around you and into the shadows beyond.

Turn to **135**.

### 157

At the cost of 1 WILLPOWER point you create a glow of light from your Staff. To your left you see a huge number of Shadakine swordsmen locked in combat with a smaller group of Guildsmen. The Shadakine are relentlessly forcing the Guildsmen back into the forest. Suddenly a hail of Shadakine arrows arcs towards you falling just short of where you stand.

If you wish to extinguish your light, turn to **344**.
If not, turn to **357**.

### 158

You peer into the wild fire at the slanted, inhuman eyes. They are closed; their penumbral grey lids a vague, tinted outline. Slowly, lazily, as if awakening from a deep sleep, they open revealing two great pools of impenetrable darkness; vast, eddying whorls of eternal shadow. The eyes beckon with a hypnotic stare, a cloaked welcome to hell's darkest and most desolate chamber.

'Who dares?' demands a slithering, deathly voice. 'Who dares to knock upon the door to the Pit of Eternal Pain?'

You stagger back as a blast of colossal psychic power, a will of great violence and malice makes your head reel and your thoughts tumble. A burning beam of thought is thrust painfully into your mind, searching, probing, searing.

'Who? . . . Who? . . .' hisses the disembodied voice. The desolate eyes are tinged with red. Savage laughter rings in your ears. 'Can this be?' the voice crows, scornfully. 'Oh! but this is the sweetest, the richest, of ironies. It is the Shianti slave, is it not? Upon the errand of fools, treading the path of the foolish? And that worthless bauble of theirs, you have found it? Yes, I see that you have.'

As the voice mocks, its power over you lessens. You know that you must resist now before you are enslaved forever.

If you have 2 WILLPOWER points, and wish to use them to resist the mastery of the being in the portal, turn to **167**.

If you do not have 2 WILLPOWER points, or do not wish to use them, turn to **176**.

## 159

Walking up to the huge doors, you lay your hands upon them and probe them with your mind. You have a vision of two brawny men pulling a thick rope attached to a metal weight in a chamber on the right of the archway. This must be how the door was opened. The use of this Magical Power has cost you 1 WILLPOWER point.

If you have the Magical Power of Sorcery, and wish to use it to trigger the mechanism, turn to **83**.

If you have learnt the higher magick of Thaumaturgy, and wish to use it, turn to **122**.

If you do not have either of these powers, or do not wish to use them, turn to **115**.

### 160

With Tanith at your side, you stand and wait for the demon charge. It is a brave but foolish decision. The demons number almost a hundred and you cannot hope to stand against them. After a valiant defence, in which many demons are slain, you fall.

Your life and your quest end here.

### 161

Owing to the speed at which you are galloping and the creature is diving, you will have enough time for only one round of combat. If you have recently drunk a Potion of Invulnerability or have the protection of invulnerability through the previous casting of the higher magick of Thaumaturgy, ignore all ENDURANCE points lost by yourself for the duration of the combat.

Winged Demon:

COMBAT SKILL 20     ENDURANCE 31

If you kill the creature in one round of combat, turn to **178**.

*(continued over)*

If you and the winged demon are still alive after one round of combat, turn to **184**.

## 162

At the cost of 1 WILLPOWER point, your power of Prophecy reveals that you are standing in the middle of intense evil. Danger is close at hand. You tell Tanith what you have learned. She nods as if this confirms what she already feared.

'We stand upon the Lissan Plain,' she says gloomily. 'Once a beautiful country, now inhabited by demons in the service of Shasarak.' With a shudder, you gaze upon your new surroundings.

Turn to **239**.

## 163

With a wild flurry of blows you triumph at last, only to be confronted with many more slavering beasts thirsting for your blood. The entire horde throws itself against you. You seem doomed to fail when Tanith's cry alerts you to a movement beyond the ridge overlooking the basin.

'My brothers; they come,' shouts Kuna. 'We are saved.'

Cresting the rise is a long line of tall, black-skinned warriors: men of the Masbaté. They send up a loud cry before releasing a volley of javelins into the rear ranks of the demon horde, killing many. The demons are thrown into disarray. Their anguished screams echo throughout the basin as the Masbaté charge down the slope with their swords drawn. The two forces collide and a short but bloody battle ensues.

Many of the demons vanish magically. Those that remain are mercilessly slain. When the battle is over, a Masbaté warrior sheathes his sword and walks towards you.

Turn to **100**.

## 164

The power required to lift so many into the air is considerable and you have never attempted this spell before. Concentrating all your energy and thought, you will the loathsome creatures to rise. With startled shrieks they drift up, gibbering and thrashing their limbs uselessly. Beads of perspiration form on your forehead; your temples throb. The demons drift fifty feet into the air before your concentration breaks and you release your hold on them. They drop like stones, hitting the ground with a sickening thud, and dying instantly. Your shoulders sag; you feel physically and mentally drained. Owing to the large effort involved, you must lose 6 WILLPOWER points and 2 ENDURANCE points.

Turn to **99**.

## 165

You draw out the Gem, filling it with mental energy drawn from the Astral plane. If you have the Magical Power of Sorcery, you use 2 WILLPOWER points; if you are versed in the higher magick of Thaumaturgy, you use 1 WILLPOWER point. The Mind Gem gives off a red glow. You use its power to reach out to the Shadakine rider and will him to you.

Turn to **186**.

## 166

You and Tanith squeeze into the alcove and keep very still. The scratch and scuffle of clawed feet tells you that the demon horde is ascending the stairs in the hall below. Soon you hear the sound of movement nearby. Peering out of the shadows you see a hunched, three-legged creature enter the chamber. A single yellow eye looks out from the centre of a broad, furrowed forehead, crested with many long feelers like antennae. The demon emits a moan of displeasure on finding the chamber empty and turns to leave. You give a quiet sigh of relief and suddenly the demon halts and begins to sniff the air, head cocked to one side with a quizzical gesture. Then it sees you and, with a feral scream, stumbles forward, its clawed hands outstretched. You cannot evade this combat and step forward into the light.

Demon: COMBAT SKILL 16    ENDURANCE 19

If you win the combat, turn to **183**.

## 167

Using 2 WILLPOWER points, you shake off the power that held you and push it from your mind.

'You cannot resist, Shianti slave,' the voice spits. 'You know not who you defy. Know you that I am Agarash the Damned, Demon lord of Darkness. You cannot stand against me. Come, come to me. Take my place here in the Pit of Eternal Pain and I shall be freed.'

You feel the force of Agarash's will once again. It is a strength mightier than any you have ever known. You fight with a Demon lord, a servant of

Naar, King of the Darkness, a force of ultimate evil. Legend tells that Agarash was once a ruler in the world of Magnamund, till he was defeated by a magical race called the Elder Magi and banished to another plane, doomed to remain there for all eternity. Agarash seeks to draw you towards the portal of fire that is the doorway to his prison.

If you wish to duel with the will of Agarash, and have 5 or more WILLPOWER points, turn to **192**.

If you wish to try to close the portal of fire using the Moonstone, and have 5 or more WILLPOWER points, turn to **209**.

If you do not have 5 or more WILLPOWER points, turn to **176**.

## 168

You triumph at last but, to your horror, you see the remaining ape demons slay your Simar steed and begin to feast on its flesh. Many miles lie between you and the pass. Those miles consist of flat, rolling grassland totally devoid of cover. The demon horde draws closer, almost snapping at your heels. There is no time to stop and prepare some magic to help you. You have no choice: you turn and run with all the speed you can muster.

Turn to **210**.

## 169

You close your eyes and concentrate. At the cost of 1 WILLPOWER point you reach out with the power of your mind. You sense a dark evil: attack is imminent. You are able to ascertain that the attack will be attempted by many and that your potential assailants

**170**

are not human, but possess an alien intelligence. Everything about them indicates a malevolent power, and it is likely that they have a limited knowledge of magic.

> If you wish to continue in the direction you are heading, turn to **213**.
> If you wish to head towards the source of evil in exactly the opposite direction, turn to **9**.

**170**

Looking up through a gap in the trees, you see a number of Winged Demons circling. They must be searching for you. Reluctantly you move on again, following the trail until you reach the far side of the forest. You hear the snapping of dead branches and the rustling of leaves: the demon horde are somewhere in the forest, searching for you. Your mind races as the growling and howling of the pack draws closer. It is vital that you find some way of drawing the pack on, towards the Shadakine Army that is moving towards Lanzi and the Masbaté who guard the bridge there. You estimate that the army must be half-way there by now, probably following the line of the River Dosar to protect its left flank. If you are seen at the head of the demon horde, you are sure to be attacked by the Shadakine.

Suddenly you sight a figure on horseback. It is a Shadakine warrior scouting the land. He must be an out-rider from the Shadakine Army. A plan begins to form in your mind.

> If you have a Mind Gem, and the power of Sorcery or Thaumaturgy, turn to **165**.

If you are versed in the higher magick of Telergy, and wish to use it, turn to **133**.

If you have the Magical Power of Enchantment, and wish to use it, turn to **108**.

If you prefer to stand and reveal yourself to the warrior, turn to **311**.

### 171

A lethal beam of force streaks towards the beast but, unfortunately, it is just off-target, exploding into a cloud of orange flame in the sky. The use of this magical attack has cost you 2 WILLPOWER points. The creature is now upon you, its great claws outstretched towards you.

Turn to **161**.

### 172

The miles pass by slowly. Though the Lissan Plain is monotonously flat and should be retatively easy to cross, the fierce heat of the afternoon sun drains your strength. Tanith looks very tired. You decide to rest and you both stop beneath the shade of a large, solitary tree. As Tanith wipes sweat from her brow she turns and gives you a searching look. 'Have you noticed?' she says.

You have no idea what she means and tell her so. 'There are no birds, no beasts, no wild creatures of any kind,' she replies.

Her observation explains the strange stillness of the plain and adds to the sense of evil that pervades it. Suddenly Tanith jumps to her feet. 'Look!' she cries 'Something is moving out there.'

You look in the same direction. In the distance you can see a small figure moving at speed, though it is too far away for you to be able to distinguish any details. The figure is moving south.

If you wish to investigate, turn to **222**.
If you wish to continue on your way, turn to **257**.

### 173

You loose a bolt of energy that spirals towards the rider. Unfortunately the rigours of your escape have left you fatigued and your concentration is not good. The attack goes wide and the horseman is unharmed. Your ill-aimed attack has cost you 2 WILLPOWER points. He is almost upon you now and you brace yourself to receive the charge.

Turn to **269**.

### 174

At the cost of 2 WILLPOWER points, you hurl a splash of lethal magical flame at the heads of the leading demons. With agonized shrieks, three of them fall to the ground. The horde falters on the stairs in an uproar of startled howls and screams. Before they can gather their wits, you rush along the gallery and down the stairway to confront the pack where they stand in confusion.

Turn to **119**.

### 175

You raise your Staff and fire at the bridge. The cost of this attack is 9 WILLPOWER points. If you do not have 9 WILLPOWER points then you must use ENDURANCE points at a rate of 2 ENDURANCE points for every 1

WILLPOWER point you lack. (ie 2 ENDURANCE points = 1 WILLPOWER point).

If you are still alive after this attack, turn to **252**.

## 176

You are weak and tired and lack the mental strength to resist the incalculable might of a Demon lord. Effortlessly Agarash takes hold of your mind, possessing you utterly. He summons you towards the portal and, like a puppet, you obey. While Agarash looks on, laughing maniacally, you pass through the gate of doom, the doorway to damnation, to a realm of nameless and eternal horror.

Your quest has failed; your adventure is over.

## 177

You take up the Moonstone and, focusing your power, gaze into it. The impenetrable blackness that formerly filled the stone disperses and a light kindles there. Soon the stone is filled with spinning colour. The spinning stops and you are looking at the Lissan Plain. Four creatures come swiftly into view. Each creature is horribly misshapen: the leading creature is a large, toad-like being with glistening green skin and a long tail. All four lope, hop and shamble along as their ghastly forms allow. There is a menacing purpose to their walk and you are sure that you are their prey. The use of this vision has cost you 2 WILLPOWER points.

If you have the Magical Power of Necromancy, and wish to use it to chant an incantation against evil, turn to **146**.

*(continued over)*

If you wish to continue moving and perhaps escape your pursuers, turn to **213**.

If you wish to head towards your pursuers, turn to **9**.


## 178

A lethal blow from your Staff strikes the demon's bony skull. It crumples and drops to land in a cloud of dust. The beast is dead. The pace of your Simar steed does not falter as you continue across the plain towards the demon portal in the hills of Tilos.

Turn to **142**.


## 179

You unleash a beam of magical fire that hurls one of the creatures to the ground in a blaze of smoke and flame. This attack costs you 2 WILLPOWER points. A commotion of shrieks and wails breaks out and the evil beasts rush away from you in fear. Some vanish into thin air, intimating the dark magic of their nature.

Turn to **53**.


## 180

You bring down the Staff to deliver a death blow but, as you do, Agarash shouts out. 'No! This shall not be.'

You feel a wave of power emanate from the wall of fire and your Staff grows warm in your hands. Both your Staff and Shasarak's explode into flame, to fall in ashes on the floor. Shasarak begins to crawl on his hands and knees towards the fiery wall, muttering in choked breaths. 'You shall not have me. You shall not have me.'

He stands and reaches out his hands. 'Agarash, our bargain!' he screams. Agarash laughs once more. A plume of flame snakes out from the wall and wreathes itself around Shasarak.

If you wish to allow Shasarak to step through the flaming wall, turn to **350**.

If you have 3 WILLPOWER points and wish to fill the Moonstone with your power and hurl it against the wall, turn to **316**.

### 181

The power of Physiurgy gives you the ability to manipulate most of the prime elements of matter, though you can never create them yourself. After a brief pause while you gather your powers of concentration, you focus on the stone door, twisting the natural shape of the stone and tugging at the atoms and molecules of which it is made. A series of cracks and fractures appears and soon it collapses in pieces at your feet. The use of this higher magick has cost you 2 WILLPOWER points.

Turn to **156**.

### 182

At the cost of 2 WILLPOWER points, you throw a well-aimed beam of force at the Winged Demon. Your uncanny accuracy inflicts a fatal wound in the creature's head and it plummets from the sky. The pace of your Simar steed does not falter as you continue across the plain towards the demon portal in the hills of Tilos.

Turn to **142**.

## 183

A final blow fells the creature. As it falls lifeless to the ground, three reptilian beasts appear in the doorway. Many more creatures crowd behind them in the corridor outside. The only possible escape from the Masbaté tomb is through the entrance to the hall five floors below. Somehow you must fight your way down.

If you wish to attack the demons standing in the doorway with a long-range shot from your Wizard's Staff, turn to **189**.

If you wish to charge the demons, turn to **219**.

## 184

The Winged Demon arcs and wheels, spiralling up into the air and preparing for another attack. It has suffered a large, weeping wound from your last attack and its flight path is erratic and slow. It gives a wailing, defiant screech and dives at you once more. If you have recently drunk a Potion of Invulnerability or are protected by the earlier casting of the higher magick of Thaumaturgy, ignore all ENDURANCE points lost by yourself during the combat.

Wounded Winged Demon:
COMBAT SKILL 15    ENDURANCE 12

If you kill the creature, turn to **178**.

If you and the Winged Demon are still alive after one round of combat, turn to **214**.

## 185

You peer down into the darkness of the well, and, at the cost of 2 WILLPOWER points, you summon up a tall, swirling waterspout. On the tip of the waterspout is a large, clay bowl. Tanith reaches out and takes the bowl and you allow the waterspout to subside with a great splash.

Turn to **25**.

**186** – *Illustration X (overleaf)*

Unsuspecting, the warrior rides towards you. He wears a plumed helmet of black metal and you know that underneath the helm his head is shaven, except for a long, plaited pig-tail. Like all Shadakine, his most notable feature is his eyes, which are completely white, without iris or pupil. He is clad in the furs and steel of the Shadakine and carries a spear. A crossbow is slung over his back.

If you still have your Simar stallion, turn to **37**.
If it has been killed, turn to **45**.

**187**

Your heart pounding, you wait as the gibbering, snarling creatures approach. As they draw closer, they move more slowly until finally they lapse into a cowering, nervous creep. Your stand obviously intimidates them, for although you are gripped with fear, you display a confident menace. Suddenly they fall upon you in a wild, slavering flurry of kicks, blows and bites.

Turn to **264**.

**188**

The Demon Master is weakening. Suddenly, in a desperate bid to escape the dazzling blur of magical

X.  Unsuspecting the Shadakine warrior rides towards you

flame that wreathes its body, it spreads its wings, and attempts to fly out of range. In that instant you swing a tremendous blow at the monster's heart. With a terrible roar, it convulses in mid-air, arms flung out and clawed fists clenched with pain. It drops like a rock. Before you are able to dodge aside, the creature's body falls directly on top of you, hurling you to the ground with terrific force. You lose hold of your Wizard's Staff and it clatters on the stone floor, just out of reach. You try to drag yourself from under the dead weight of the Demon Master but, dazed and confused by the fall, you are unable to scramble free.

Tanith rushes forward to grab your Staff. As she does, the demon minions that surround you let out a pealing cry of crazed glee and surge forward. Tanith manages to pick up the Staff before being forced to back away. She holds her dagger before her in readiness but against so many she cannot hope to prevail. Slowly she edges towards you. The Staff is tantalizingly out of reach. Tanith dares not turn her back on the advancing horde to give it to you. The position looks hopeless. Then, amid the whirl of your thoughts, you hear the cries of human voices and the clash of steel. You turn to look in the direction of the sound. Pouring through the entrance of the tomb comes a mass of tall warriors, swords bared, reaping a deadly harvest amongst the demonic ranks.

Turn to **38**.

## 189

Raising your Staff, you unleash a beam of fire that tears into one of the creatures. It screams horribly as it falls dead in the doorway. The remaining creatures give vent to pealing cries of fear and begin to edge backwards, their twisted features writhing. This attack has cost you 2 WILLPOWER points.

Turn to **219**.

## 190

You throw the light of the Moonstone against Shasarak. He recoils in pain, then straightens, producing a long, black Staff from thin air. With a hideous scream he charges at you, his Staff whirling, rage contorting his already twisted features.

If you wish to exert 1 WILLPOWER point to continue the protection of the Moonstone, turn to **307**.

If you wish to meet Shasarak's attack with your own Staff, turn to **323**.

## 191

With a whirl of colour, you find yourself in a long, grey hall. You guess that you are close to Shasarak for at the far end of the hall you see a door engraved with a large Shianti rune representing Shasarak's name. Guarding that door is a grotesque creature, a servant of Shasarak. It is a demon, summoned from some ghastly netherworld that only the dark sorceries of Shasarak could reach. The demon has a high, humped back and a square, flat face that bears two blank, emotionless eyes; colourless and entirely lacking in any warmth or feeling; like pebbles by an unknown sea.

'Hail, enemy of my master,' it breathes, 'I have waited for you. My master told me you would come.'

You step closer. With some concern you see that the

demon has affected the shape of a man, with blonde, gilded hair. You tell yourself that this is no man, but a demon in human guise. The demon stands tall; it mocks. 'Why have you delayed? What are your reasons? I have waited so long . . . so long to meet your challenge. I am powerful, I am mighty! Know you, that I am the Ipagé, greatest of all demons under my master's command. My power is that of hate, for, indeed, I hate you, free and unstained as you are, unheeding of the powers that I and my master hold most dear.'

The creature's tirade of scorn is unrelenting and, to you, quite meaningless. It does not hate you, but what you represent; the wild, free, unrestrained wisdom of the Shianti. Shasarak has taught it that this wisdom is meaningless. You know that this is a wisdom, not born of knowledge, but of the freedom of the spirit, of the soul to follow its own way, sure that a mind without hate or resentment can do no harm. The Ipagé hisses like a serpent as you approach. You notice that its body is transparent and shimmers with an eerie light. The door to Shasarak's chamber lies directly behind this evil guardian. So far it has made no attack.

If you wish to attack this creature of hell, turn to **296**.

If you wish to ignore it and head straight for Shasarak's door turn to **39**.

### 192

You struggle desperately, but you fight a creature with the power of a god: you cannot hope to master it. Your will snaps and Agarash draws you towards the portal. You move like an automaton, a mindless zombie. To the sound of Agarash's cackling laughter, you step through the portal into eternal doom and damnation, a realm of nameless horrors.

You have failed, your quest is over.

### 193

You rain a torrent of blows on to the heads of your attackers at the cost of 2 WILLPOWER points and a wide space around you is soon filled with the dead bodies of your assailants. Before the survivors are able to close once again, you dig your heels into the stallion's flanks and it starts away like an arrow from a bow. The demons try to pursue but the fleet-footed Simar steed is too fast for them and they soon disappear from view.

Turn to **142**.

### 194

You close your eyes and send the power of your thought into the stone. Eventually you locate a system of weighted pulleys on the left-hand side of the doors. Now that you know where the mechanism is, you will be able to use another of your Magical Powers to open the doors. The use of this Magical Power has cost you 1 WILLPOWER point.

If you have the Magical Power of Sorcery, and wish to use it to trigger the mechanism, turn to **83**.

If you have learnt the higher magick of Thaumaturgy, and wish to use it, turn to **122**.

If you do not possess either of these powers, or do not wish to use them, turn to **115**.

## 195

You close your eyes and concentrate your mind on the far bank of the river where you can see King Samu urging his brave soldiers on. At the cost of 2 WILLPOWER points you teleport, experiencing the sickening feeling that always accompanies teleportation. You appear on the other side of the river and at Samu's side. He looks round and sees you.

'By the Gods!' he shouts, raising his sword to strike you.

You remember that you are still wearing the Shadakine uniform.

If you wish to pull off the Shadakine helm and show Samu who you are, turn to **280**.

If you wish to raise your Staff to defend yourself from Samu's blow, turn to **308**.

## 196

Using the power of Sorcery, you will be able to create a wall of energy that will act as a barrier or forcefield. However, the shield will only be as strong as the amount of WILLPOWER you put into it and it cannot be moved like a conventional shield. Remember, if you wish to use your Wizard's Staff, you will have to drop the shield.

If you wish to use 1 WILLPOWER point to create the shield, turn to **278**.

If you wish to use 2 WILLPOWER points, turn to **291**.

If you decide not to use the Magical Power of Sorcery for protection after all, turn to **102**.

### 197

The hovering Spiderfly drops from the air as your final, fatal blow slips past the eight-legged screen of the creature's defence. But there is no time to celebrate your victory. A large number of the horde have reached the top of the valley and are now only a few hundred paces further along the ridge. You have very little time in which to attempt to close the portal before the demons, who number more than twenty, reach you.

Turn to **139**.

### 198

You summon your mental energy and focus it on the half-running, half-hopping leading demon. There is no time for hesitation: you throw your thought at the creature. With a startled yell, it floats into the air, limbs waving uselessly. Stunned, the demons that follow come to an abrupt halt, gibbering insanely and pointing at their hideous companion as he drifts above their heads. With an easy motion, you fling him down. He lands with a sickening thud on top of his fellows, sending them sprawling to the ground.

They scramble to their feet, cowering and backing away in fear. You step forward with a threatening gesture, but they do not wait to see your next move. Faster than an eyeblink, they vanish into thin air. You are safe. The use of this Magical Power has cost you 2 WILLPOWER points.

Turn to **99**.

### 199

With split-second timing you dodge aside, avoiding

the oncoming chariot. It thunders past, then turns into a skid and crashes. The men inside are thrown screaming into the air. With a grim smile of satisfaction, you return to the army camp. There you see that the Guildsmen, while ready to leave, hesitate before the forest. Sado shrugs with resignation. 'They are afraid to tread within the eaves of the forest,' he says.

Turn to **343**.

## 200

The night passes without incident but you are wakened at dawn by the sounds of scratching and scrabbling from below. The sinister murmuring of distant voices echoes ominously throughout the vast hall and the hair on the back of your neck prickles with fear at the sound of a low, bestial moan, alien and chilling. Tanith wakes with a nervous start. Sensibly she says nothing, but her dagger is in her hands in a moment, her eyes flashing dangerously, her body taut. Slowly you edge out of the chamber and peer through the supporting columns of the balcony. In the golden glow of the dawn light that creeps through the shafts of the roof, you are confronted by a nightmarish vision.

The floor of the ziggurat is a heaving carpet of horror. A swarm of hideous creatures lurks there, gibbering insanely. Each wears a different and equally misshapen guise: toad beasts, their green hides glistening, crawl beside stunted anthropoids with matted fur and scabby flesh; creeping reptiles with human heads vie with many-limbed crustaceans; lurching serpents slither upon the backs of hulking beetles. Never before have you seen such a ghastly horde of evil deformity.

'The demon plague,' hisses Tanith, horrified. 'Such was the evil that defeated the brave Masbaté. Who could stand against such fearful monstrosity?'

The shuffling column reach the foot of the stairs. With every passing moment more are entering the ziggurat through the gateway that you yourself opened but could not close. Now it is you that must attempt to stand against the demon plague. Five floors below, a terrifying doom approaches. The demons advance, slowly, cautiously, unsure of their new environment. Certainly, they are unaware of your presence in the highest gallery of the ancient Masbaté tomb. You have little time in which to plan an escape.

> If you are versed in the higher magick of Necromancy, and wish to use it to begin an incantation to ward off evil, turn to **113**.
> If you wish to attack the demonic horde with your Staff at long range, turn to **137**.
> If you prefer to try to hide, turn to **151**.

## 201 – *Illustration XI*

A faint splash startles you into awareness. In the darkness you can make out the dim outline of a boat heading towards you. 'Hail the shore,' a voice whispers out of the darkness.

You stand, Staff held aloft, ready for combat. 'Who calls?' you call into the darkness. There is no answer but soon you are able to discern a tall figure, standing upright in a large, wooden rowing boat. He

XI. 'Hail the Shore!' a voice whispers out of the darkness

draws closer and, to your amazement, you find yourself looking upon a giant of a man, perhaps seven or more feet tall with long, flowing hair and skin as black as ebony. You realize that this man is a Masbaté warrior, member of the tribe believed by all to be extinct.

'I witnessed your struggle with the demons from the shore', he says. 'Come, more are sure to return soon, and in greater numbers. You must come with me. You are not safe on this side of the river.'

You and Tanith clamber aboard the boat and, with strong strokes, the warrior rows you to the other side of the river. There, a great host of Masbaté warriors wait. You can hardly believe your good fortune at this timely rescue or that members of the great Masbaté people still exist. You have only ever known one Masbaté: Samu, a noble and fearless warrior, who accompanied you on your search for the Moonstone. Once he was king of the Masbaté nomads but he thought himself the only survivor of his people. Everyone believed that the Wytch-king, Shasarak, hounded them into extinction, sealing their doom with the unleashing of the demon plague.

'I am Dioka,' says the man who has rowed you ashore. I am leader of the warrior band that patrols the banks of the river in the defence of the Masbaté. Who are you?'

You regard the Masbaté host with a joyful expression. 'Greetings, men of the Masbaté,' you call, ensuring that all can hear. 'I am the Wizard, Grey Star, bound upon a quest in the service of the Shianti and sworn to the destruction of the Wytch-king, Shasarak.'

Wide-eyed, the Masbaté regard you with stunned expressions. 'Can this be?' Dioka gasps, shaking his head in disbelief. 'If this is true, then you must tell the king. Will you accompany us to the Kashima Mountains, where we of the Masbaté now dwell?'

You nod your agreement. 'Then come.'

Soon you are struggling to keep pace with the fleet-footed warriors, heading through the dark shadows of night towards the mountains: the secret lair of the last of a proud and mighty race.

Turn to **260**.

### 202

With a silent prayer, you break into a swift gallop: somehow the Simar stallion senses the need for speed. The flying horrors ahead spread out into a diagonal line. The first of the line, a Flying Snake, begins its dive towards you. You swerve to one side at the latest possible moment, forcing the creature to bank and turn half-way into its dive. Claws and talons outstretched, the Winged Demon swoops towards you once more. You cannot evade combat.

Flying Snake: COMBAT SKILL 19    ENDURANCE 18

Combat lasts for only one round as the creature flashes past. If the Flying Snake loses more ENDURANCE points than you, ignore any ENDURANCE points you lose.

If you are still alive, turn to **226**.

### 203

The Magical Power of Thaumaturgy grants you many powers but many of the magical feats you are able to perform are costly in WILLPOWER. You must decide the best way of using this power.

If you wish to make yourself invulnerable to physical attack, turn to **91**.

If you wish to levitate, turn to **132**.

If you wish to cause *all* the demons to levitate, turn to **164**.

If you wish to cause *one* of the demons to levitate, turn to **198**.

### 204

At the cost of 2 WILLPOWER points you release a blast of energy at the first few ranks of the demon host. You slay three, but the demons number in their hundreds and a loss of three does not delay or deter them. Together they give vent to a ferocious scream that echoes all around the valley as they charge towards you.

If you have recently drunk a Potion of Invulnerability, or have the protection of the higher magick of Thaumaturgy, and you wish to stand and receive the charge of the demons, turn to **104**.

If you do not have this protection, and wish to stand and receive the charge of over four hundred crazed beasts thirsting for your blood, turn to **94**.

If you wish to escape attack, turn to **233**.

## 205

At the cost of 2 WILLPOWER points you throw a bolt of magical flame at the nearest of the hideous creatures, a hairless ape with a tough red hide. It stumbles with a squeal of pain and drops its gruesome burden. A discontented murmur spreads through the demons' ranks and suddenly they begin to run in the opposite direction, heading for the stairs that lead to the hall.

Turn to **107**.

## 206

Though mortally wounded, the winged ape holds on grimly. Then, suddenly, it hurls itself away, still holding the stallion's harness. The horse's head is twisted violently to one side and the noble animal loses its balance, tumbling to the ground. You lose 2 ENDURANCE points in the fall.

If you are still alive, turn to **272**.

## 207

Without slowing your steed's thundering gallop for an instant, you ride down a wailing, two-headed beast with mottled skin and rubbery feelers. Other beasts scatter in a cloud of dust, blood and flashing hooves. You sweep past the demons in a matter of moments. They attempt to pursue you but your fleet-footed Simar steed is too fast for them. Eventually the demons slip out of sight.

Turn to **142**.

## 208

With a gasp you cease your attack: you are nearly unconscious with the strain. Staggering slightly, you look up to see the doors still standing. Your attempt has failed. A few minutes pass before you feel steady on your feet.

If you have the Magical Power of Thaumaturgy, and wish to use it to open the doors, turn to **295**.

If you have the Magical Power of Elementalism, and wish to summon an elemental to open the doors for you, turn to **289**.

If you have learnt the higher magick of Physiurgy, and wish to use it, turn to **181**.

If you do not possess these powers, or wish to return to your earlier journey towards Lake Dolani, turn to **234**.

## 209

Your body trembling with the effort of concentration, you hurl power into the Moonstone and direct it towards the portal. The portal burns with white-hot intensity and the eyes of Agarash burn deep into your heart. For, while you concentrate your power on the portal, you are undefended from Agarash's attempts to master you. The stallion rears and turns in absolute terror and your head screams insanely, but you never waver from your attempt upon the portal. The malice of Agarash fills your body and tears at your soul, yet still you hold the glowing gem aloft, clinging to it with fierce resolve. There is a mighty explosion and Agarash's frustrated scream echoes for miles around. The portal has been destroyed and Agarash can no longer reach you: you have escaped damnation at his hands. You have exerted 4 WILLPOWER points and must lose 3 ENDURANCE points.

Even as the portal is destroyed, Agarash's last words

thunder around the valley. 'Minions of Agarash, slaves of the scarlet fires – destroy! Destroy and avenge me!'

If you are still alive, turn to **268**.

## 210

At first you make good speed but you are heavily laden and your Staff and Backpack hamper movement. The snarling and screeching behind tell you that the demon host is beginning to gain on you. You chance a look over your shoulder and see that some of the faster-moving demons are separating from the main group and are very close. Three reptilian beasts with clashing fangs are soon snapping at your heels.

If you wish to turn and fight these three, turn to **302**.

If you would prefer to continue, turn to **315**.

## 211

You close your eyes and cast an illusion, using 1 WILLPOWER point. You transform yourself into a giant, writhing serpent and slither towards the demons. They hesitate for only a moment before continuing to charge towards you. The illusion has failed. These are magical creatures, immune to the Magical Power of Enchantment.

Turn to **264**.

## 212

You dismount, hoping that the horse does not stray, and plant yourself squarely, feet apart, to face the oncoming rush of Winged Demons. They are travelling at an incredible speed. Your heart is pounding. You mutter a Shianti prayer of hope under your breath and concentrate on the flock of creatures, judging their speed as closely as you can. You notice that they are spreading out into a kind of battle formation: a diagonal line angled towards you.

If you wish to fire a long-range attack with your Wizard's Staff at the leading demon in the formation, and you have 2 WILLPOWER points, turn to **317**.

If not, turn to **244**.

## 213

You continue on your easterly course, constantly on the look-out for danger. More than an hour of tense silence passes as you and Tanith hurry along. The tension is broken by Tanith's sudden cry. 'Look!' she says, pointing. 'There's a river up ahead.'

Less than a mile away, a river gleams and sparkles. You and Tanith break into a trot. When you reach the river bank you both drop to your knees, bending to scoop up great handfuls of cool water. You drink long and deeply before your raging thirst is quenched.

You have reached the banks of the Dolani River. It leads south and fills Lake Dolani, which lies at least thirty miles away, according to Tanith. To the north east lie the Kashima Mountains, where the river begins; the mountains look to be at least fifty miles away. The river is too wide and too deep to cross at this point; you will have to travel further upstream where it is likely to be narrower and shallower.

You are just bending to take another drink of the

refreshing water when Tanith touches you lightly on the shoulder. 'Grey Star,' she murmurs. 'Ready yourself. We are about to be attacked.'

Turn to **227**.

## 214

Only just alive, the creature lands on the ground with a faint cry. Before you are able to finish it off, it disappears from view. No doubt it has teleported to the portal in the hills of Tilos. You dig your heels into the stallion's flanks and it surges forward, renewing its unfaltering gallop across the grassy plain.

Turn to **142**.

## 215

Holding the Moonstone aloft, you descend the stairs adjoining the galleries. As you reach the last, you come face to face with the demon horde. In the passage before you stand three reptilian beasts, hunched, malformed figures with yellow, glistening fangs and red, baleful eyes. As the first rays of the Moonstone touch them, the protective aura of your necromantic spell causes them to shield their deformed faces and howl in torment. With horror, you notice that the demons behind them are dragging the corpses of the Masbaté dead from their crypts. The three before you snarl and spit in frustration, hovering just beyond the range of the protective ring.

If you wish to attack at long range, with your Wizard's Staff, turn to **179**.

If you wish to advance on the demons, turn to **53**.

### **216** – *Illustration XII*

You run through the shadowy darkness and emerge at the forest's edge, where Shadakine and Freedom Guild swordsmen are locked in bloody combat. The Shadakine have the advantage of greater numbers and are forcing the Guildsmen into the forest in a stumbling, disorderly line. They cannot hold for long. You suddenly realize that the strange, pupiless eyes of the Shadakine allow them to see in the dark. No wonder they have attacked in the middle of the night. Their advantage is considerable. A tall officer stands behind the Shadakine warriors, urging them on. Your sudden appearance at the edge of the forest has startled him but he quickly recovers. He bares his teeth and snarls before attacking.

Shadakine Officer: COMBAT SKILL 20    ENDURANCE 24

If you wish to evade, you may do so now by darting back into the undergrowth; turn to **290**.

If you win the fight, turn to **301**.

### **217**

Using the power of Telergy, you attempt to dominate the will of the creatures and throw a word of command at them. Although you succeed in halting them, you notice that they are all attempting to resist your command. These creatures must be magical and immune to most forms of enchantment. However, the power of Telergy is a higher magick, unknown to all but the highest masters of the magical arts and suddenly the demons vanish. Unable to prevent the domination of their minds, they have

XII.    The Shadakine and Freedom Guild swordsmen are locked
in bloody combat

fled, using their own magical powers. You are safe. The spell has cost you 2 WILLPOWER points.

Turn to **99**.

## 218

Fearlessly you spur your horse into a downhill gallop, ploughing into the ranks of the leading beasts and scattering bodies everywhere. The momentum of your charge carries you deep into their midst but, inevitably, the pack's large number absorbs the shock of your attack and you find yourself hemmed in on all sides.

If you have recently drunk a Potion of Invulner-ability, or have the protection of the higher magick of Thaumaturgy, turn to **104**.

If you do not have this protection, turn to **94**.

## 219

With an impetuous cry, you rush forward, whirling your Staff above your head. The demons stumble backwards in alarm, careering into those behind and causing an uproar of animal cries. With a deadly flash of steel, Tanith fells one of the beasts with her dagger, and, at the cost of 1 WILLPOWER point, you deliver a powerful blow that sends another crashing to the ground. You reach the doorway of the crypt. The demons are running in the opposite direction, heading for the stairs that lead back down to the hall. Horrified, you notice that some are dragging the corpses of Masbaté dead from the crypts.

Turn to **107**.

## 220

You loose a bolt of enery at the horseman, using 2 WILLPOWER points. A cloud of fire explodes at his chest and he falls from his horse, dead. You run to the body. By stealing the dead horseman's uniform, you will be able to lead the demon host against the Shadakine Army; the Shadakine will think that you are one of their own.

If you still have your Simar stallion, turn to **285**.
If it has been killed, turn to **292**.

## 221

Taking careful aim at the leading demon, you hurl a bolt of magical fire, killing it instantly. The horde comes to a stumbling halt. This attack has cost you 2 WILLPOWER points.

The Masbaté reach you. Without stopping to ask who you are, they release a volley of shining javelins that arc over your heads and plunge into the demon ranks. Swords drawn, the Masbaté sprint past. You and Tanith are swept along by the momentum of their charge and into the throes of a bloody battle. You almost collide with a hunched, ape-like creature with four arms and a long tail. You cannot avoid combat and must fight to the death.

Ape Demon: COMBAT SKILL 18   ENDURANCE 17

If you win the combat, turn to **150**.

## 222

You head south in pursuit of the lone figure. Soon you have drawn close enough to be able to see that the figure is humanoid in shape, although it runs with a curious, shambling gait. The shimmering heat haze prevents you from discerning any further details. Abruptly it comes to a halt. You quicken your pace. Tanith has begun to lag behind but offers no word of protest. Purposefully you stride towards your prey, but stop dead in your tracks when you come within fifty paces of it.

Turn to **110**.

## 223

You skid to a halt and try to judge how much time you have before the demon host in the west will reach you. You guess at a quarter of an hour at most. But first you must survive the onslaught of the denizens that speed towards you.

If you wish to fight on horseback, turn to **277**.
If you wish to fight on foot, turn to **212**.

## 224

You veer sharply, heading west for a while. Soon the figures have passed out of sight and you are able to resume your course towards the hills of Tilos.

Turn to **237**.

## 225

You walk around the building but cannot find a water hole or stream. The west wall of the ziggurat bears a ten-foot high arch. The doors are made of stone.

'How are we to open these?' asks Tanith.

You guess that there must be some internal

mechanism for opening the doors. They are certainly too heavy to be opened by hand.

If you have the Magical Power of Prophecy, and wish to use it to find an opening mechanism for the doors, turn to **194**.

If you have the Magical Power of Psychomancy and wish to use it to find an opening mechanism, turn to **159**.

If you are versed in the higher magick of Thaumaturgy, and wish to try to teleport yourself to the other side of the doors, turn to **148**.

If you have none of these powers, or do not wish to use them, turn to **18**.

### 226

Before the next demon dives, you begin an erratic sequence of diagonal moves. The demons are thrown into confusion and you are able to reduce the distance to the pass. When at last the next dive comes, you are taken by surprise. Instead of attacking you, the winged Demon gouges a line of bloody weals along the stallion's haunches. The stallion screams in pain but does not falter. You chance a look behind and see that the horde is still far away. A third demon dives. This beast has an insectoid body combined with feathered bird's wings. You attempt a dummy turn but the beast is not fooled.

Insect Demon: COMBAT SKILL 18    ENDURANCE 17

Combat lasts for only one round. If your enemy loses more ENDURANCE points than you, ignore any ENDURANCE points you lose.

If you are still alive, turn to **265**.

## 227

Four distant forms mount a rise that slopes gently away from the Dolani River. As they head towards you, you see that they are ghastly, malformed creatures. Each is misshapen in a different way. These must be the demons summoned long ago by the Wytch-king, Shasarak, and sent as a plague to destroy the Masbaté tribe that once dwelt here. When the demons' purpose was fulfilled they were left to roam the plains at will.

The leading demon, its shining green skin and toad-like features reflected in the dull glow of the setting sun, gives vent to a feral scream and begins to run towards you.

If you have the Magical Power of Necromancy, and wish to use it to chant an incantation against evil, turn to **35**.

If you wish to attempt a long-range attack with your Wizard's Staff, turn to **65**.

If you prefer to wait for the demons to approach, turn to **93**.

## 228

The remaining Flying Snake keeps pace with you for a short while longer before soaring into the air and disappearing from view, heading east.

Turn to **247**.

## 229

You hand Tanith your Staff and Backpack and begin to climb into the uncertain darkness of the well. Half-way down one of the rungs comes loose in your hand. You are unable to keep your balance and fall, hitting the sides of the shaft many times and enduring many cuts and abrasions before splashing into the water below: lose 1 ENDURANCE point.

Gasping for breath, you reach out blindly in the dark until you locate a large, bowl-shaped object. Having made sure that it is full of water, you begin the slow, arduous climb to the top, struggling to hold on to the rungs and the bowl of water. Eventually you reach the top and Tanith takes the bowl from you. Bruised and bedraggled, you haul yourself out.

Turn to **25**.

### 230

The Shadakine are wheeling large engines of war to the front of their lines: they are powerful catapults. Pin-points of flame appear. Sado has guessed their intentions and orders his bowmen to fire. The archers of the Freedom Guild send volley after volley singing through the air towards the Shadakine and many of the distant spots of light go out. Suddenly many balls of flame arc through the air above the heads of the men of the Freedom Guild to fall into the trees behind.

'Hah!' Sado shouts. 'The fools are way off target.'

'I think not,' replies Samu.

You understand his meaning as you watch the dry brush of the forest begin to burn. 'They mean to flush us out!' you cry with alarm.

All around you small fires are catching the trees and in a short time smoke billows in choking clouds throughout the Freedom Guild's ranks. Orange tongues of flame are licking on every side.

Turn to **351**.

## 231

As the group draws nearer, you realize that these are the horrific forms of demons. Half-man and half-beast, with slavering fangs and sword-sharp tusks, they run towards you. They come within a hundred paces, their cackling yells and feral howling indicating that they mean to attack.

If you wish to charge, turn to **246**.
If you wish to attack them at long range with your Wizard's Staff, turn to **258**.

## 232

While your enemies are dazed, you charge forward, whirling your Staff above your head. The demons are too stunned to react and suddenly you are upon them, raining deathly magical fire in all directions.

Turn to **264**.

## 233

You tug the stallion's head to one side and pull away from their shambling advance at a gallop. You skirt the edge of the valley, keeping a large distance between yourself and your enemies. They fall into babbling confusion, splitting into disorganized groups and making their various ways out of the valley. You move at great speed, faster than the confused mass that seeks you out, and you cover the mile in a short time, thundering to a halt at the other end of the valley where the portal burns half-way down the slope.

As you study the burning arch, a large, winged spider with eight bulbous but distinctly human eyes swoops towards you. It is coming at you too swiftly for you to be able to fire at it from long range and you cannot evade without risking serious injury. It is a fight to the death. If you have swallowed a Potion of Invulnerability, or used the higher magick of Thaumaturgy to render yourself invulnerable, ignore all ENDURANCE points lost by yourself for the duration of the combat.

Demon Spiderfly: COMBAT SKILL 25    ENDURANCE 24

If you win the combat, turn to **197**.

### 234

You continue at an even faster pace in your bid to find the lake before nightfall. Your throat is parched and the exertion of walking in such heat causes you to lose 1 ENDURANCE point. You notice that the plain is beginning to slope gently upwards.

If you have the Magical Power of Alchemy, or are versed in the higher magick of Theurgy, turn to **241**.

If you do not possess either of these powers, turn to **43**.

### 235

The large Flying Snake hurtles towards you. You hold your Staff aloft and brace yourself to receive the attack but the stallion is nervous and unsettled and you are unable to remain in any one position for very long. Also, you are forced to use one hand to control your mount. You cannot evade combat and must subtract 2 from your COMBAT SKILL for the duration of the combat.

Flying Snake: COMBAT SKILL 21    ENDURANCE 24

Combat lasts for only one round as the demon swoops past. If your enemy loses more ENDURANCE points than you, ignore any ENDURANCE points you lose.

If you are still alive, turn to **313**.

### 236

You run along the gallery and down many stairways to confront three reptilian beasts. Hunched and mal-formed, the creatures have glistening fangs and baleful eyes. Before you are able to take any further action they hurl themselves at you emitting blood-curdling screams. You cannot avoid combat and must fight to the death.

Three Demons: COMBAT SKILL 18    ENDURANCE 24

If you win the combat, turn to **245**.

### 237

Judging from the position of the sun in the blue, cloudless sky, you estimate that it is well past noon when the green hills of Tilos come into view. There has been no further sign of the demon plague. The protection of the Moonstone and the aura of light that you have summoned with your necromantic powers must have kept the demons at bay. Where then are they? Samu told you that there are possibly a thousand of the evil creatures. Surely they will seek to prevent you from reaching the portal that is the sole gateway to their world?

If you are versed in the higher magick of a Visionary, and wish to expend 2 WILLPOWER points in its use, you must give up the protection from evil granted to you by the use of the higher magick of Necromancy, since both spells require the use of the Moonstone. If you wish to cease your use of the power of Necromancy and use your power as a Visionary, turn to **249**.

If you have the Magical Power of Prophecy, and wish to use it at the cost of 1 WILLPOWER point, turn to **266**.

If you do not possess either of these powers, lack sufficient WILLPOWER points to use them, or do not wish to use these forms of magic at the moment, turn to **271**.

## 238

You ride the horse to the edge of the river and dive in. You swim with desperate strokes, but the Shadakine armour drags at your body.

Pick a number from the *Random Number Table*. Add this number to your current ENDURANCE total.

If the total is *12* or less, turn to **80**.
If the total is more than *12*, turn to **86**.

## 239

Mountains lie all around you on the horizon. You guess that it is summer, for the sun beats strongly and the sky is cloudless. Despite the heat, Tanith shivers. 'There is an evil presence here,' she mutters.

According to Tanith, you have arrived in the centre of the Lissan Plain. The fortress city of Shadaki lies many hundreds of miles to the east. A broad line of distant mountains separates you from that city of evil. Suddenly you realize that you have no food or water. The simplest of requirements stands between you and the fulfilment of a quest upon which thousands of lives depend. If you do not find water soon you will die.

If you wish to head east in the direction of the city of Shadaki, turn to **172**.

If you wish to head south, turn to **60**.

## 240

Your journey proceeds without further incident. You can see the wide, forested pass a few miles away. Once you have gained the safety of the trees, you will wait for the demon host to seek you out, and then make a final dash for the Lanzi bridge on the River Dosar, where Samu and the Masbaté will be waiting for you. But your spirits have lifted too soon. Heading straight towards you is a dark cloud of wings and snakelike bodies. It is a flock of flying snakes, numbering at least twenty.

If you wish to try to make a dash for the forest, turn to **101**.

If you wish to make a stand, turn to **261**.

## 241

A flash of colour catches your eye: it is a collection of purple Phinomel. This flowering shrub, also known to some as Dragonkiss, grows round the base of rocks and stones, taking root in the damp soil beneath. The name Dragonkiss comes from the plant's curious, perilous flowers. Each flower is a semi-transparent pod and its colour comes from the potent, purple acid within each one. If the main plant is disturbed the pods may squirt a stinging jet of acid, capable of inflicting a painful burn. If the pods can be plucked carefully from the main plant, without disturbing the main plant, the acid can be preserved and used at a later date. The acid is of great use to Alchemists and Theurgists as a constituent part of a formulae to transform base metals to metals of greater worth.

If you wish to pluck some Phinomel pods, turn to **4**.

If you wish to continue on your way, turn to **43**.

### **242** – Illustration XIII (overleaf)

The moon bursts through a space in the clouds and you see Sado, a bloody sword in one hand, standing upon the brow of a low hill. He and a small number of his personal guard are beset on all sides by Shadakine warriors. You sprint over to him. Looking to the east, you see a sight that makes you gasp, Beyond the edge of the forest is the Shadakine Army. It is larger than you ever imagined, row upon row of bristling spears and swords wink beneath the night sky. Among the ranks you sight the glow of a Kazim Stone; a Shadakine Wytch must accompany the army.

You enter the battle that rages at Sado's feet in an effort to free him so that he can command the rest of the army. More and more men appear out of the darkness, summoned by his rallying call. A Shadakine

XIII.    Sado stands upon the brow of a low hill, a bloody sword in his hand

spearman springs out of the shadows and runs towards you.

If you have 2 WILLPOWER points and wish to fire at the spearman at long range, turn to **324**.

If you wish to stand and face the warrior's charge, turn to **330**.

If you wish to flee, turn to **335**.

### 243

A second blast of flame sends another demon to its doom; the hunched creature with a shiny purple back, shaped like a beetle lies in a heap on the ground. With a mad gibber of panic the others de-materialize. You are safe. This magical attack has cost you 2 WILLPOWER points.

Turn to **99**.

### 244

A large Flying Snake hurtles towards you. You hold up your Staff and brace yourself to receive the attack. The beast's razor-sharp talons flex and stretch to scour your flesh. You cannot evade combat.

Flying Snake: COMBAT SKILL 20   ENDURANCE 20

Combat lasts for only one round as the demon flashes past. If your enemy loses more ENDURANCE points than you, ignore any ENDURANCE points you lose.

If you are still alive, turn to **287**.

### 245

With an awful shriek, the last of the demons falls dead at your feet. There are more behind but they back away cautiously, spitting and growling. With horror, you notice that many of the demons are dragging the corpses of the Masbaté dead from their crypts.

If you wish to attack one of these demons at long range with your Staff, turn to **205**.

If you wish to charge the demons, turn to **154**.

### 246

You dig your heels in the stallion's flanks and it launches into a thunderous gallop. You come within ten paces of the demon line; the light from the Moonstone, which you hold aloft, shines brightly on their faces. With the first touch of its rays, the pack emits a chorus of wailing and anguished shrieks. They scatter in all directions, shielding their grotesque faces and squirming to avoid the Moonstone's light. However, before your charge can hit home, they disappear: they must have teleported to the portal in the hills of Tilos. You slow the white stallion and proceed at a gentler pace.

Turn to **237**.

### 247

Something appears in the clear, sunlit sky. At first you think that one of the little winged snakes has returned, but, as the creature draws closer, you realize that this beast is far larger, though identical to the earlier serpents in every other way.

If you wish to attack the Flying Snake at long range with your Wizard's Staff, turn to **66**.

If not, turn to **59**.

## 248

Still levitating, you drift towards the demon as it prepares to launch itself at Tanith. At a height of ten feet, you release the spell and fall on to the creature's back. It crashes to the ground with a piping scream and you roll away from its inert body and flip back on to your feet. Glowering, you face the remaining demons, who begin to edge back, gurgling with fear. Sensing your advantage, you loose a terrifying cry and launch yourself at them, Staff ablaze. The demons freeze, panic-stricken, but before you can strike they vanish. You are safe.

Turn to **99**.

## 249

You gaze into the Moonstone and, using 2 WILLPOWER points, you fill the orb with visions of nearby events. The swirling haze of colours clears to reveal a deep valley. At the bottom of that valley you can see a multitude of demonic creatures. They stand before a shimmering arc of fire that hovers in the air. This is the demon portal; they lie, waiting for you to approach.

Turn to **274**.

## 250

Somewhere in the forest your pursuers are stamping through the dense foliage, smashing their way towards you. You leap into the saddle of the Shadakine mount and speed away, heading south towards Lanzi, where Samu and his Masbaté warriors are waiting for you at the bridge. You pray that the Shadakine Army is already well on its way to Lanzi.

Glancing over your shoulder you see the first of the horde burst from the undergrowth of the forest. You concentrate on the last frantic dash that lies ahead of you.

Turn to **352**.

## 251

The shadows have deepened into night as the last demon falls dead at your feet. Despite the unfavourable odds, you have triumphed. Tanith is unharmed but you are exhausted after your efforts. Panting, you fall to your knees, head slumped and shoulders heaving as you regain your breath.

Turn to **201**.

## 252

You remain conscious long enough to see the bridge erupt into flames and collapse into the waters of the River Dosar. Then you faint with exhaustion into Samu's arms. When at last you come round it is night and the Masbaté have made camp along the route towards the Army of the Freedom Guild in the south.

Turn to **321**.

## 253

Hurriedly you run along the gallery in search of a place to hide. A babble breaks out from the creatures below: you have been spotted. The scuffle of webbed and clawed feet tells you that the demon horde is rushing up the stairs towards you. There is nowhere to hide. The only way down to the hall is by those stairs and you may only leave the tomb by the entrance to the hall.

'We'll have to fight our way out,' you say to Tanith. She nods, a grim expression on her face.

Turn to **236**.

**254** – *Illustration XIV (overleaf)*

With quaking heart, you ascend the hill. You stand at the top in a circle of stone forms with the indistinct features of men. Their voices murmur in a haunting, faraway whisper.

'He comes . . . the Grey One comes . . . '

'Does he bear the key . . . the Masterstone . . . our salvation?'

'Who are you?' you shout into the darkness. The whispering subsides and one voice speaks to you.

'We are the Kazim; the Stone peoples. Old as the earth. We have waited.'

'For what?'

'For the bearer of the Masterstone to set us free from this hill that we might claim back what was once ours. We seek our hearts that the Dark One stole from us long ago.'

A glimmer of realization dawns in your mind. 'Who?' you ask, urgently. 'Who stole your hearts?'

'He who calls himself Shasarak, sundered and shameful brother of the Shianti.'

The Kazim Stones of the Shadakine Wytches must be the hearts of these poor, forlorn creatures. Trapped

XIV.   'We are the Kazim. The Stone peoples. Old as the earth.
We have waited'

and heartless upon this hill they have waited for you to free them. 'But how?' you ask the Kazim.

'You must have the key or we would not have awakened from our sleep of centuries and felt your presence here in the forest. You are the bearer of the Masterstone. Take it out and free us as the Shianti promised.'

They must mean the Moonstone. Long ago the Shianti must have promised to free the Kazim out of shame for the actions of their renegade Shianti brother. Now you have come to fulfil that promise for them. The Kazim mentioned regaining their hearts. If they are successful, they rob Shasarak's most powerful servants of their power. The separate threads of the story fall into place as the ancient plans of the Shianti finally come to fruition. You draw out the Moonstone. Though you have not exerted any power upon it, it is shining with a blinding white light of its own. The seven Kazim roar with pleasure as the rays of the Moonstone touch their rocky bodies, and then they begin to move, stretching their craggy limbs after centuries of sleep.

One of the Kazim speaks to you. 'We thank you,' it says. 'But you must go now, back to your people. Their enemy approaches, bringing with them an enemy of ours. We will come soon, when we are fully ready and restored to life. Hurry. Battle begins.'

In the distance you can hear the sound of many voices shouting. The Shadakine must have attacked by night. You whirl around and dash down the hill, heading towards the sound of battle.

Turn to **358**.

## 255

Taking a deep breath, you plunge a point of concentrated sorcery into the doors. As the beam of energy hits the fabric of the stone, you realize that you will need to use a great deal of WILLPOWER before the doors will break. With a huge surge of energy you throw 5 WILLPOWER points at the door.

Pick a number from the *Random Number Table*. If you have the Magic Talisman of the Shianti, add 2 to the number you have picked.

If the total is 4 or more, turn to **283**.
If the total is less than 4, turn to **208**.

## 256

You charge towards the Shadakine ranks facing the bridge. They are surprised by the unexpected attack from behind, especially as it seems that they are attacked by one of their own kind. In a kind of mad desperation, you attempt to force a passage through the swirling mass, pulling off your helmet to show the Masbaté on the bridge that you have returned. There are a great number of Shadakine standing between you and the bridge. You must fight them as one enemy and to the death. Owing to the initial surprise of your charge, you may add 3 to your COMBAT SKILL for the duration of this fight.

Shadakine Warriors:
COMBAT SKILL 22    ENDURANCE 40

If you win the combat, turn to **353**.

## 257

You continue east. When you next look over your

shoulder, the figure has vanished. An uneasy feeling stirs inside you. You quicken your pace. As the sun slowly crosses the sky, the heat becomes less intense and walking becomes easier. Nevertheless, you grow more anxious as the evening approaches for you have seen no trace of a stream or water hole and you will never find one at night. You can survive without food for some time but you must find water soon.

If you are carrying the Moonstone in your hand, turn to **81**.

If you are carrying it in your Backpack, turn to **213**.

## 258

A plume of fiery light shoots from your Staff and hits a two-headed man shape with a black horn in the centre of each brow. It falls dead, wreathed in magical fire. The nine that remain continue to shamble towards you but, when they have come within ten spaces, they suddenly scatter in all directions, shielding their grotesque faces and twisting to avoid the light of the Moonstone. The next moment they have vanished, teleporting to the portal that lies somewhere in the hills of Tilos. Your magical attack has cost you 2 WILLPOWER points.

Turn to **237**.

## 259

The chariot careers along a wild and unpredictable course. Desperately you try to judge its next turn as it bears down upon you.

Pick a number from the *Random Number Table*. Add this number to your current ENDURANCE total.

If the total is *12* or more, turn to **199**.
If the total is less than *12*, turn to **263**.

The night has grown old before you arrive at the torchlit entrance to a cave in the Kashima Mountains. Dioka leads you through a maze of winding passageways in the rock and eventually you come to a wide cavern. At the far end of the cavern, mounted on a rough-hewn dais of stone is a large throne. Sat upon the throne is the Masbaté king deep in thought, his hand cupping his broad jaw. Suddenly your heart lifts. You recognize this man!

'My lord,' Dioka begins. The king lifts his great head. 'May I present!'

But the sentence is never finished, for the king is none other than Samu himself. 'Grey Star!' he cries, rising to his feet. 'You live!'

Before you can speak a word, King Samu leaps from the stone dais and bounds towards you, sweeping you up in a bone-crunching embrace. 'Seven years, Grey Star,' he booms. 'Seven years since last we stood together. We thought that you perished long ago, deep in the caverns of Desolation Valley. What became of your search for the Shadow Gate of the Daziarn – did you succeed after all? Did you find the Moonstone of the Shianti? What has happened since you stepped upon the wasted lands beyond the Lissan Mountains?'

He hugs you once again, squeezing the air from your lungs. When you have regained sufficient breath to speak, you explain what has happened to you since you were separated, and of how the passage of time runs differently on the Daziarn plain. 'I have but recently returned,' you say. 'And behold!' You draw out the Moonstone. 'I succeeded. Look you upon Shasarak's bane – the Moonstone of the Shianti.'

A great noise fills the hall as the Masbaté warriors clash their weapons and call out their battle cries. The Moonstone blazes with a vivid white light that illuminates the whole hall and the faces of the fierce Masbaté. Samu draws his own sword with a great cry. 'The final battle begins,' he bellows. 'Revenge will be ours. Death to the Shadakine! Death to the Shadakine Wytches . . . and death to the Wytch-king, Shasarak, foe of the Masbaté and the Shianti, enemy of all life itself!'

The great chamber echoes with the ferocious cries of the Masbaté warriors. When the clamour has died down, you and Tanith are led to chambers within the mountainside, there to eat and rest. The following morning you will meet King Samu to discuss ways in which the Masbaté can aid you in your struggle against Shasarak. You drift off to sleep that night with your spirits lifted. Tomorrow you must ensure the safety of the Army of the Freedom Guild before the Shadakine force, due to move in two days, is able to march against it. You know now that you will not have to face that peril alone.

Turn to **298**.

## 261

You brace yourself to receive the first of the fearsome beasts, a large Flying Snake. You watch as it gains sufficient height for its dive. The stallion prances nervously, shifting this way and that; it is difficult to control.

> If you wish to release a long-range attack at the Flying Snake, and have 2 WILLPOWER points, turn to **111**.
>
> If not, turn to **152**.

### 262

Suddenly the wounded creature gives vent to a maniacal screech and all four throw themselves at you. Staff swinging, you rise to meet their challenge, a lone figure besieged by hell-borne minions of insane ferocity.

> Turn to **264**.

### 263

The chariot is veering crazily. It is impossible to judge which way it will swerve next. It turns abruptly and heads towards you. Your senses are slow to react and you are unable to move quickly enough to avoid the oncoming rush of the chariot. You are trampled to death by the horses.

Your adventure ends here.

### 264

With an energy borne of sheer desperation, you send a volley of blows at the beasts with your Wizard's Staff. You cannot evade combat.

Four Demons of the Plains:
COMBAT SKILL 21    ENDURANCE 34

If you win the combat, turn to **281**.

## 265

Two more attacks follow on the stallion rather than yourself. Its pure white coat is stained with blood and you can feel its pace begin to falter.

You see a small, winged ape circle above you and shoot downwards. At the last moment it slows its descent, grabbing hold of the horse's harness and tugging it violently. You struggle and twist in the saddle and try to aim a blow at the gibbering creature without falling from the horse. The stallion stumbles but does not fall.

Winged Ape: COMBAT SKILL 22    ENDURANCE 16

If the combat lasts for three rounds, turn to **206**.
If you win the combat in one or two rounds, turn to **68**.

## 266

At the cost of 1 WILLPOWER point you close your eyes and concentrate. Your senses reach out and search. In the hills beyond, a terrible evil waits, a malevolent, unthinking, yet strangely natural evil. A dark force lies in wait for you! You are expected.

Turn to **274**.

## 267

Tense with anticipation, you wait for the lone figure to arrive. It is humanoid in shape and you notice that it moves with a strange shambling gait. Suddenly it comes to an abrupt halt . . . and vanishes! A thrill of fear runs down your spine: There is an unfamiliar magic at work. Tanith gives you a questioning look but says nothing. With a shrug you continue on your way, the mystery unresolved.

Turn to **36**.

### 268

Even as Agarash's words are fading, a tumultuous roar fills the air: the demon host is roused into a frenzy. Instinctively the Simar steed turns and thunders up the slope of the valley, heading east. The howling pack springs forward in pursuit, possessed of a savage fury instilled in them by their master. The terrified stallion flies like the wind out of the Tilos hills and on to the even plain. The countryside rushes past in a blur of green. Now you must head for the pass in the mountains to the east, a patch of forest among the hills.

Almost fifty miles lies between you and the pass. You look over your shoulder to see that the enraged beasts are beginning to dwindle in the distance as the Simar's broad, rolling gait eats up the miles. The horse's coat gleams with sweat and there is foam around its mouth but it no longer moves with the madness of a runaway.

If you wish to stop for a while, turn to **31**.
If you wish to continue as you are until you reach the pass, turn to **47**.

### 269

The horseman thunders towards you. You brace yourself.

Shadakine Horseman:
COMBAT SKILL 19    ENDURANCE 20

Combat lasts for only one round, as the speed of his charge carries him past you.

If you kill the horseman, turn to **17**.
If not, turn to **33**.

### **270** – *Illustration XV (overleaf)*

The dark, fearsome shape stands before you, towering at least ten feet high. It has the head of a large bull and wisps of smoke curl from its flaming nostrils. Its eyes burn with a terrible intensity that fills your heart with dread as it lifts its horned head and roars. It stretches its broad bat wings, throwing a cloak of shadow over you. The demons that fill the hall are but minions of this fierce master. Before you are able to summon magical forces to combat this awesome foe, the Demon Master lunges forward on its cloven feet. Its grasping, clawed hands reach out, hungry to squeeze the life from your body. You may not evade this combat.

Demon Master: COMBAT SKILL 30    ENDURANCE 40

If you defeat the Demon Master in three rounds or less, turn to **188**.
If the combat lasts for four rounds, and you are still alive, turn to **276**.

### **271**

Moving at a slow trot, you journey into the hills. After travelling for half an hour or so you hear a low murmuring of strange, inhuman voices. As you crest the next hill, you find that you are looking down a gentle slope that leads into a shallow valley. With horror, you see that the floor of the valley is a crawling

XV.  The Demon Master lunges forward on its cloven feet

writhing mass of demons. Never before have you seen such a damnable pit of diabolic malevolence. Every conceivable distortion of human and animal life waits there, grotesque combinations of many different beasts.

A thousand corrupt faces look up at you where you sit, mounted on the great white stallion, atop the highest ridge of the valley. Even the stolid nerves of the Simar steed are shaken and it stamps and snorts in distress. A sinister moan of disquiet ripples through the ranks of the cursed creatures. It is a dreadful sound. You sway in the saddle, such is the force of such a concentrated pool of evil, all focused upon you. An unconquerable tide of fear wells up inside you.

If your current WILLPOWER total is 20 or more, turn to **284**.

If your current WILLPOWER total is less than 20, turn to **44**.


### 272

Bruised and bleeding, you drag yourself to your feet. The stallion is dead. A knot of panic stirs in your belly. Many miles of flat grassland devoid of cover or protection lie between you and the pass. Without stopping to ponder your sad loss you turn to run.

Turn to **210**.


### 273

Boldly you head towards the distant figure.

'Take care, Grey Star,' Tanith cautions.

The distant figure runs with a curious, shambling gait. As you advance to meet it, your body tingling with apprehension, it comes to an abrupt halt. Several paces later you also stop dead in your tracks.

Turn to **110**.

## 274

Using this Magical Power, you are able to sense the exact location of the demon portal: it lies in the valley at the centre of this range of hills.

You journey for less than half an hour and, below the crest of the next hill, you dismount and lead the white horse with all the stealth you can muster. You move along the perimeter of the hill's ridge until you come to the far end. Then you peer over the lip of the hill and down its gentle slope. You look upon a shallow valley covered with a crawling, writhing mass of utter horror. Every conceivable malformation of human and animal life waits there, grotesque combinations of many different beasts. A wave of revulsion washes through you. A shimmering arc of fire hovers in the air about three hundred yards down the slope: it is the demon portal that only you can close.

If you have a Potion of Invulnerability and wish to swallow it now, turn to **294**.

If you do not have such a Potion, or do not wish to use it, turn to **134**.

## 275

Suddenly the night sky is filled with fireballs, hurled from Shadakine catapults. They fly through the air above the heads of the Army of the Freedom Guild and land in the trees behind them. The dry brush of the forest begins to burn.

'They mean to flush us out!' you cry alarmed.

All around, fires are starting. Soon the surrounding trees are ablaze. Smoke billows in choking clouds through the ranks of the army, and the fire is still spreading.

Turn to **351**.

## 276

Despite your brave resistance, the Demon Master seems to be drawing on hidden reserves of power. Suddenly its leathery wings flap and it lifts into the air with deceptive speed. The surprise movement catches you off your guard and the hoof that lashes out at your head throws you to the stone floor. Blood streams from a wound in your forehead: lose a further 3 ENDURANCE points. Your senses whirl from the force of the blow.

If you are still alive, turn to **20**.

## 277

You brace yourself to receive the first charge of a Flying Snake, watching it as it ascends to a sufficient altitude for the maximum impact on diving. The stallion prances nervously and your heart hammers at your ribs.

If you wish to release a long-range attack at the Flying Snake, and have 2 WILLPOWER points, turn to **304**.

If you prefer not to, turn to **235**.

## 278

Drawing on the force of your will, you shape a wall of sorcerous energy in front of you. You use 1 WILLPOWER point. The toad-like demon slams into the magical wall with a squawk of disbelief. It stares stupidly at the shimmering shield, touching it with its fingers. Before you can take any further action, it disappears into thin air along with its three companions. You relax your guard for a few moments and then suddenly the four demons reappear. Only now they are positioned behind you and the sorcerous wall is useless. With a malicious shriek of glee, the four demons pounce.

Turn to **264**.

## 279

Cautiously you enter the hill country of Tilos. You have been wandering for an hour when you hear a suspicious sound like a distant murmur. Coming to the top of a hill, you look out on to a shallow valley. At the bottom of the valley is a crawling mass of horror: hundreds of demons lurk there. Parts of many beasts exist in grotesque combinations, a perverse mockery of nature's laws. Hundreds of corrupted faces look up at you sat astride the great white stallion upon the highest ridge in the valley. Even the stolid temperament of the Simar steed is shaken. It stamps and snorts, obviously distressed. A sinister moan of disquiet ripples through the creatures' cursed ranks. You sway in the saddle, recoiling from the malice focused on you. At the far end of the valley, less than a mile away, a shimmering arc of fire hovers in the air: it is the portal. It is too far away for you to be able to close it from here, and the entire demon plague stands in your way. A commotion breaks out below, and the demons begin to edge their way slowly up the valley towards you.

If you have a Potion of Invulnerability, and wish to drink it now, turn to **8**.

If not, turn to **121**.

## 280

Hurriedly you pull off the helmet and stand flinching beneath Samu's poised sword. But he is an expert warrior and he checks its downward sweep in an instant. His eyes bulge in amazement. 'Grey Star!' he gasps. 'I almost killed you!'

'No time . . . no time,' you reply, quickly, shaking Samu from his stupor. 'Call your men; we must retreat. See?' you say, gesturing across the river. 'I have brought the demon plague. We must flee while they and the Shadakine fight.'

It is as you say. Across the river the demons wage a ferocious battle against the Shadakine. Instantly Samu springs into action, calling to his men and ordering a trumpeter to sound a retreat. The Masbaté retire. The Shadakine are too involved in their fight to pursue, at least for the moment, but you know that it is essential to destroy the bridge to prevent any pursuit should the Shadakine, who must number in their thousands, quickly defeat the demon plague.

If you have the Magical Power of Elementalism, and wish to use it, turn to **314**.

If you are versed in the higher magick of Physiurgy, and wish to use it, turn to **7**.

*(continued over)*

If you are versed in the higher magick of Thaumaturgy, and wish to use it, turn to **26**.

If you do not possess any of the above powers, you must attack the bridge with your Staff; turn to **59**.

## 281

When at last the fury of the battle has passed, you look down and see the lifeless corpses of the demons. Unbelievably, in the face of such overwhelming odds, you have triumphed. Exhausted by the effort of your defence, you drop to your knees, panting heavily. Eventually Tanith's efforts rouse you, and you resume your journey east.

In the dim light of night, you see a sparkle in the distance. It is a river. Both you and Tanith break into a run, only stopping, breathlessly, to drink its cool waters. You have drunk long and deep before your thirst is quenched. Tanith expels a breath of satisfaction, sitting up on her haunches and wiping her mouth with the back of her hand. She scours the land.

'I'd guess that this is the Dolani River,' she says. 'It leads south, where it fills Lake Dolani about thirty miles downstream. Upstream, its source is somewhere in the Kashima Mountains.'

To continue your journey east, you will have to cross this river. It is too wide and deep to wade across here and the current is too fast for swimming. The river is likely to be narrower and shallower as it nears its source.

Turn to **201**.

You continue the journey. At noon you cross the River Anduis near the town of Sena. You stop to warn the townspeople of Sena of the advance of Shadakine forces and enlist their help in destroying the bridge. This will ensure that the garrison at Andui, and the larger army beyond the River Dosar, will have to cross the River Anduis at the bridge of the city of Andui.

By late afternoon you can see the large and mysterious Forest of Fernmost looming in the west. You have made good time. The Masbaté are tireless runners and have kept pace with your horse with little effort. You are passing a group of hills beyond the boundaries of the dark forest when you see a group of horsemen riding towards you. Each of them wears a red veil, part of the uniform of the Army of the Freedom Guild. When the riders are within a hundred paces, they stop and aim their bows at you.

'Hail there men of the Freedom Guild. We are friends. Put down your weapons,' you shout.

'Who calls himself friend, yet marches from the north before an army?' questions one of the riders.

'I would speak with your leader, Sado of the Long Knife,' you reply. 'Tell him an old friend has returned to aid him. Tell him it is I, Grey Star, of the Shianti.'

At these words, the horsemen lower their bows and look at you in amazement as you ride towards them. You now wear your grey Shianti robe once more. Their expressions become joyous. 'You have come. You have returned,' they cry. 'Sado said it would be so but none believed.'

With glad hearts, the horsemen lead you and the Masbaté to the Freedom Guild's camp, which lies a few miles south of the hills. You come upon a sprawling mass of tents and fluttering banners. The camp is alive with activity. As you and the Masbaté pick your way among the tents and the campfires you attract a great deal of attention. Some soldiers offer a rousing cheer at the sight of the size of the Masbaté host: useful reinforcements in a time of desperate need. You and Samu leave the Masbaté to pitch their own camp in an unploughed field nearby and go to Sado's tent together. The tent flap is pulled aside and Sado of the Long Knife steps out. You recognize his lean, haggard and dangerous blue eyes. These eyes soften and a smile breaks across his face when he sees you.

'Grey Star, I knew you would come back,' he says. 'Hail Samu, and welcome.' You both exchange greetings with the brave leader of the Freedom Guild. Inside his tent you tell him of the success of your quest for the Moonstone and the warning words of the Shianti, when they spoke to you in the chamber of the Moonstone.

'And so,' you say to close your story, 'it is their wish that we fall back into the Forest of Fernmost to escape the larger Shadakine Army that is sure to come against us once they have crossed the Dosar and Anduis rivers.'

Sado's brow furrows. 'But the forest is a place of evil,' he says. 'Perhaps foul creatures of Shasarak's lurk there – creatures that would be his slaves if he desired it. Surely it would be better to march on Suhn and take it by siege. Once we occupied it, we would have a stranglehold on the bulk of Shadakine trade. It is the only port foreigners will visit in the Shadakine Empire, and its city walls would offer a better defence.'

'The Shadakine host would reach you before the Port of Suhn could be reduced,' you tell him patiently. 'And they outnumber your army three to one. You would be cut off from your base at Karnali and the Shadakine would be able to send reinforcments by sea. You would lose Karnali for sure and the whole seat of the rebellion would be destroyed, and your army too.'

Sado looks doubtful. 'My army numbers ten thousand men. All are well trained. Your long absence has not seen us idle. We have engaged Shasarak's slaves wherever we have found them and my soldiers are well tested in combat.'

The argument lasts well into the night, but Sado's faith in you, the Moonstone that you bear, and the wisdom of the Shianti, of whom you have spoken, eventually persuade him. Preparations are made to move the army out the following morning.

Turn to **354**.

### 283

A tumult of stones and rock shards falls noisily to the ground as the door cracks and then collapses. You nearly faint with the exertion of breaking the door and your head throbs but you have succeeded.

Turn to **156**.

## 284

You look into the lambent glow of the Moonstone, shining forth with unquenchable purity. Your fear subsides. At the opposite end of the valley, less than a mile away, a shimmering arc of fire hovers in the air: it is the portal of the demon plague. You will never be able to close the portal at this distance. You must get closer. But the demon plague stands in your way. Though your aura of protection keeps them at bay, you know that you will have to release this spell while you use the Moonstone to close the portal.

If you wish to ride to the other end of the valley, keeping high up on the slope away from the demons and attempt to close the portal without moving among the demon ranks, turn to **52**.

If you wish to ride into the valley through the demon horde, to stand before the portal itself, turn to **61**.

## 285

Quickly you don the uniform. Your Simar steed is exhausted and the Shadakine horse offers the chance of greater speed. You slap the Simar's haunches and watch it trot away. The beast has served you well and you offer a silent Shianti blessing that will keep the horse from harm.

Turn to **250**.

## 286

The figure is approaching from the south. There is no available cover on the open plain, so you can only evade by choosing to travel in a different direction from the figure.

If you wish to head north, back the way you came, turn to **77**.

If you wish to head west, turn to **95**.

If you wish to head east, towards the mountains that stand between you and the fortress city of the Shadakine, turn to **127**.

### 287

You brace yourself for another attack but, instead of attacking you, the Winged Demon that plunges through the air assails the stallion, gouging bloody weals across its haunches. The stallion cries frantically and you realise the flaw in your strategy. The speed of your horse is an invaluable asset: you cannot risk leaving it unprotected. You mount, ready to fly. The Simar steed canters forward, then races into a full gallop.

Turn to **265**.

### 288

At the cost of 2 WILLPOWER points you release a bolt of magical fire from your Staff. It rips into the leading demon, killing it instantly. The remainder of the pack continue to charge on. Two of their number already confront you. Tanith and Kuna stand at your side. Kuna is unarmed and Tanith has only a dagger with which to defend herself. You cannot evade combat as evading would mean leaving them to face the pack alone.

Two Demons of the Plains:
COMBAT SKILL 18     ENDURANCE 20

If you win the combat, turn to **163**.

**289** – *Illustration XVI*

You close your eyes, sinking into the trance state required for the summoning of the elementals. Chanting in their secret tongue, you send the essence of your need into the elemental plane, reaching out for the brute strength of an earth elemental. A long pause ensues after completion of the chant: Earth spirits are notorious for their slow wits. Then there is a faint tremor in the ground beneath your feet. With an explosion of rocks and soil, a huge figure rears up before you. Its body is shaped like that of a muscular human, but it is angular, sharp and hard like rock. It is a Stoneghast. A thing of granite rather than flesh, it clambers out of the chasm it has made to reach you and stands above you, a towering fifteen feet in height. Taking great pains to make your command as simple as possible, you point at the stone door of the ziggurat. 'Smash!' you shout clearly.

Wordlessly, the Stoneghast turns and walks towards the door with large, thunderous strides. In accord with the simplicity of its nature, the elemental walks straight into the door, shattering it as if it were glass. The task completed, it dives headlong back into the chasm. The earth moves to cover the Stoneghast's passing and, with a ripple, settles back into place. The use of this power has cost you 1 WILLPOWER point.

Turn to **156**.

### 290

You step back and duck down in the undergrowth. The officer charges after you but does not see you hidden behind a bush. As he stops and looks around, you leap up and hurl him to the ground with a

XVI.    With an explosion of rocks and soil, a huge figure rears up
before you

colossal killing blow. You hear Sado shouting in the distant darkness. You follow the sound of his voice.

Turn to **242**.

## 291

At the cost of 2 WILLPOWER points, you raise a shield of sorcery, forged from the energy of your will. The toad-like demon careers into it, forced to a halt with an astonished cry. When it has climbed back to its feet, it stands before the magical shield, tentatively touching the barrier with its hands. Suddenly all four of the demons vanish but almost immediately they reappear behind you, grinning maliciously. The sorcerous shield before you has been rendered useless. With an animal shriek the demons pounce.

Turn to **264**.

## 292

Quickly you don the uniform. You cast an appraising eye over the riderless Shadakine mount that stands nearby.

Turn to **250**.

## 293

With a fearsome battle cry you hurtle down the stairs and the pack scatters in all directions before you are able to inflict a single blow. The light from the Moonstone begins to fade as the power of the incantation wears off but it hardly matters now that you have cowed the hellish beasts into submission. Suddenly the horde begin to gloat unpleasantly and you halt. At the far end of the hall looms a tall shadow.

Turn to **270**.

### 294

You prepare to do battle with the demon host and decide to take advantage of the protection your Theurgic Potion offers. You swallow the dark, bitter liquid and slowly your body begins to glow with a strange blue light. Remember that the effects of the Potion will fade in a few hours. Delete the Potion of Invulnerability from your *Action Chart*. You may keep the empty vial in your Herb Pouch or your backpack. Mark your *Action Chart* accordingly.

Turn to **134**.

### 295

Tentatively at first you probe the strength of the doors with a field of mental energy, seeking out the weakest spot. Then, with a tremendous effort of will, you hurl a charge of mental energy into the stone itself. There is a rumbling as the doors vibrate with magical energy, then a resounding crack as one of the doors fractures and falls to the ground in a cloud of dust and rubble.

Pick a number from the *Random Number Table*. Subtract 1 from the number you have picked. If the result is zero, pick again, otherwise, this number is the total number of WILLPOWER points you have used in your assault upon the door.

Turn to **156**.

## 296

As though the demon can read your mind, he throws himself at you before you are able to unleash an attack at him. Your own hatred of what he represents has betrayed you; now you must fight him to the death.

Ipagé Demon: COMBAT SKILL 20    ENDURANCE 20

If you win the combat, you may pass through Shasarak's door and turn to **39**.

## 297

As you approach the building, its huge size becomes apparent. It is a magnificent structure, a towering ziggurat. As you stand before it, you realize that it is very old. The stone is weathered and overgrown with weeds and the cornerstones have been worn to ragged curves by the wind. It looks deserted – an ideal place to shelter for the night if only you could find some water. Tanith walks up and examines a section of the wall. It is inscribed with symbols.

'This was once a building belonging to the Masbaté tribe,' she says. 'They built it long ago.'

You listen with interest. The Masbaté were the original inhabitants of the Lissan Plain. The present-day king of the Masbaté, Samu, a noble and fearless warrior, accompanied you when you sought the Moonstone. But he was a king without a kingdom, for Shasarak slew all the Masbaté, unleashing the peril of a demon plague to roam the Lissan Plain. It is said that those demons roam the plain still. You find the existence of the building curious, for the Masbaté were a nomadic tribe, crossing the plain according to the seasons and the needs of their cattle. Why should they build anything so permanent?

If you wish to explore the ziggurat of the Masbaté, turn to **225**.

If you prefer to continue to search for Lake Dolani, turn to **234**.

The following morning you talk with Samu in his private chamber. You enquire after the fates of the old Kundi man, Urik the Wise, and Hugi the Thief, who also accompanied you on your quest for the Shadow Gate. You learn that Urik returned south to rejoin his people in the forests of the Azanam. Hugi, much to your surprise, returned to fight alongside Sado of the Long Knife with the Army of the Freedom Guild. Samu journeyed north from Desolation Valley to revisit his old country, the Lissan Plain. By chance he stumbled upon the surviving members of his people, who lived within the small belt of land around Lake Dolani and Lake Iss. It seems that the demons of the Lissan Plain are reluctant to cross water and so the lands beyond the rivers of the plain remained unstained by their presence. Only one pass leads out of the plain to the country that surrounds it beyond the mountains and the Masbaté held this pass against the demons. Under Samu's new-found kingship, the last survivors of the Masbaté were reunited and formed a new, though smaller, realm around the southern lakes of Lissan. They created for themselves a home within the mountains, using it as a place to hide from the malevolent eye of Shasarak. They have fought unceasingly with the demons of the Lissan Plain, which Shasarak left to roam at will after the last of the Masbaté were thought to be slain, for the Masbaté still hope to regain the whole of the plain.

'Their numbers are much reduced, compared to the great host that defeated us of old, though many hundreds still remain, especially the more powerful and cunning of their kind,' explains Samu. 'And there is a power that eludes us yet, the power that allows them to remain in the world. There is a magical gate within the hills near Lake Tilos, the gate that allowed them into the world. It was Shasarak who opened this portal for them and they are able to travel through it to their demon plane as they wish. Whenever they are attacked by a Masbaté force likely to defeat them, they can transport themselves to this portal instantly. While such an escape route remains open to them, we can never hope to defeat them entirely.'

While Samu speaks, a plan begins to form in your mind, a plan that would rid the Masbaté of the demon plague for ever and provide an answer to the problem of delaying the Shadakine Army long enough for you to warn the Freedom Guild of the overwhelming force that marches against them. You remember how the Moonstone opened a corridor from the Daziarn plane to the real world. Surely it must be able to reverse the process and close the portal in the hills east of Lake Tilos.

'If it were not for the demon plague,' Samu continues, 'and the threat it offers, we of the Masbaté would have joined forces with the Freedom Guild long ago but our wives and children must be protected. We could not leave them to the mercies of the demon plague. It is our belief that when the demons cross water they lose their ability to transport themselves to their portal. But if we warriors were not here to withstand them, they would have no need to use that power.'

'Worry no longer King Samu,' you say, as a plan crystallizes in your mind. 'I will close the demon portal and, with the help of your brave warriors, I will lure the evil demon host to the Shadakine themselves.' You explain the plan. You will journey to the hills of Tilos and, using the Moonstone, attempt to close the portal. Such an action is sure to attract every demon of Lissan against you. Then you will flee to the pass in the Kashima Mountains with the demon horde in pursuit. You will time this action so that you are able to lead the demons into the rear of the Shadakine column as it approaches the bridge that crosses the River Dosar at Lanzi.

'But how can you be sure that the Shadakine Army will not have crossed the bridge at Lanzi before you reach them?' Samu asks.

'The Masbaté must hold the bridge against the Shadakine until I can lure the demons against them,' you reply.

Samu nods in understanding. 'And who will go with you to the portal?'

'I will go alone. All of the Masbaté will be needed to hold the bridge. My magical powers and the Moonstone will protect me. They must.'

Suddenly the door of the king's chamber is thrown

open. Tanith stands there, white-faced and trembling. 'She has found me, Grey Star,' she says in a quavering voice. 'She has searched and she has found me!' Tanith looks weak; she can barely stand. Her eyes have a terrible haunted look.

'Who . . . who has found you?' you ask, fearing the answer.

'Mother Magri, my old mistress, the Shadakine Wytch of Suhn. She has searched for me with the Kazim Stone and she has found me. Long I resisted her as she tried to probe my mind. She beckons, Grey Star, she calls, I cannot resist her much longer.'

While Tanith remains, she is of great danger to you, for in seeking Tanith Mother Magri will discover that you have returned to the world. As a servant of the Wytch-king, Shasarak, Mother Magri and her power over Tanith imperils your life and your entire quest. Tanith, it seems, has realized this already.

Turn to **10**.

## 299

Only one hundred feet lies between you and the Masbaté, who are spreading out into battle formation, preparing to charge the demon horde. You will never know the outcome of the battle. Only one hundred feet from salvation the pack of evil beasts falls upon you, dragging you to the ground.

Your life and your quest end here.

## 300

The entire day passes without any sign of the

Shadakine. The army are well ensconced in defensive positions around the edges of the forest. Your sleep that night proves extremely restful, restoring 4 ENDURANCE and 3 WILLPOWER points. The following day there is still no sign of the Shadakine Army. A tense, uneasy silence descends on the men: they are anxious to fight. That night you are awakened by the crooning call of voices that beckon you.

Unable to resist, you rise and follow the sound deep into the forest. As you walk among the impenetrable shadows, you hear, mingled with the calls, the mournful creak of trees, whose branches have been stirred by a newly risen wind. You become aware of a sickly yellow glow deeper in the wood. You walk towards it, treading a path that leads up a steep hill of craggy, moss-covered stone. At the top of the hill are seven hulking shapes, tall as trees, wreathed in yellow light. The light reminds you of the yellow light of the Kazim Stones, instruments of truth and torture, power and possession, belonging to the Shadakine Wytches. A wave of panic grows inside you. The crooning is emanating from the tall forms within the halos of light, only now the words of the song are distinct:

> We are the Kazim, masters of truth,
> Wielders of power, steadfast in sooth,
> Lost are our stone hearts to the evil of the night,
> Clutched by the dark one, stealer of light,
> We wait for the Grey One, foe of the dark,
> Heralding battle, to regain our hearts.

If you wish to charge up the hill and attack the tall shapes there, turn to **339**.

*(continued over)*

If you wish to go to the top of the hill and investigate the tall shapes, turn to **254**.

## 301

You defeat the Shadakine officer with a deceptive, sweeping blow aimed at his body. You then charge at the backs of the Shadakine, taking them by surprise. Their attack falters, and the men of the Freedom Guild surge forward, driving the Shadakine before them. You hear Sado shouting to his men, attempting to rally them to him. You and the men of the Freedom Guild follow the sound of his voice.

Turn to **242**.

## 302

You come to an abrupt halt, wheeling your Staff around like a scythe. The crazed beasts are taken completely by surprise and you press home your advantage, hacking and slashing at them ferociously. You must fight them as one ememy.

Three Reptile Demons:
COMBAT SKILL 24     ENDURANCE 25

If you win the combat in three rounds or less, turn to **56**.

If the combat lasts for four rounds or more, turn to **319**.

## 303

Using 2 WILLPOWER points you fire at the chariot, aiming for one of the wheels. The wheel explodes into flames and the chariot collapses in a great cloud of dust. The men inside are hurled screaming into the air. With a satisfied nod, you turn and follow Sado and his men. Back at the camp, you see that the Guildsmen, while well ordered and ready to depart, are delaying moving to the forest. Sado shrugs. 'They are afraid of the forest,' he says.

Turn to **343**.

### 304

At the cost of 2 WILLPOWER points you hurl a ball of flame into the sky. But the nervous prancing of the stallion spoils your aim and the attack is wasted.

Turn **235**.

### 305

Using 2 WILLPOWER points you fill the Moonstone with power. As its swirling mists part, you are confronted by the haggard face of an old woman. You give an involuntary shudder; Mother Magri is staring straight at you.

'Seek and ye shall find,' the old crone jeers. 'And find her I have. Won't you come now, little one? There's plenty of room for you, my sweet.'

Abruptly the image disappears. Tanith must have been drawn back to Suhn already. There is nothing you can do for her now. You can only hope that she can survive Mother Magri's clutches until you can find a way of saving her.

Turn to **282**.

### 306

While another Winged Demon is ascending to a height from which it can dive, you turn and urge your steed to one last great effort towards the forest. At the forest's edge the plain is dotted with bushes and trees, preventing the Winged Demons from attacking. With a happy sigh you enter the leafy sanctuary of the woods. You dismount and lead the stallion along the curving trail that runs through the heart of the forest. You find a well hidden clearing, where you can rest for a few moments and plan the last stage of your task.

Turn to **170**.

### 307

He brings down his Staff, aimed to split your skull with a crushing blow. You bring up the Moonstone to meet it and the blow is deflected. Shasarak cries out with frustration. Although the Moonstone has absorbed the attack, its light is now extinguished and Shasarak turns to attack once more.

Turn to **345**.

### 308

You raise your Staff but Samu, a veteran warrior, swerves the falling arc of his blow into a side swipe that slices around the line of your defence. Only when you are slain does Samu realize the tragedy of what he has done, destroying the last hope of the Freedom Guild with one fatal blow.

Your life and your quest end here.

### 309

As the winged forms circle overhead, you trace a zig-zag pattern on the ground as you run. They swoop and dive and circle once again, but your mind is quicker. A huge, winged ape plummets towards you. Its claws find your flesh and inflict a livid wound in your shoulder. You lose 3 ENDURANCE points.

If you are still alive, turn to **62**.

## 310

A keening howl echoes round the hall, filling your ears, skull, chest and limbs and grinding the essence of your being to dust. Shasarak's might floods along the Staff, battling against your power, but you do not let go, *will* not let go, as your body trembles and shudders as though it will burst.

Add together your current WILLPOWER and ENDURANCE totals. Subtract Shasarak's score of 10 from this. (Do not adjust your *Action Chart*.)

If your score totals more than 0, turn to **5**.
If it totals 0 or less, turn to **2**.

## 311

You stand at the edge of the forest, waving your arms to attract the rider's attention. He turns and heads towards you. At first he moves at a trot but, as he comes closer, he spurs his mount into a gallop, lowering his spear and pointing it at you.

If you wish to attack the horseman at long range with your Staff, turn to **318**.
If you wish to stand and receive the attack, turn to **269**.

'Will no one follow?' you implore with searching eyes. There is a long, brooding silence, broken only by the occasional ring of armour as the guildsmen shuffle uneasily.

'Will none listen to the wisdom of the Shianti?' you shout into the silence. There is the sound of movement to your left. With relief you see King Samu striding towards you, leading a long line of his own warriors.

'We of the Masbaté will heed the words of the Shianti,' he booms. 'We at least do not fear to tread beneath the trees of Fernmost, not while a wizard of the Shianti leads us.'

You hope that Samu's words will shame the Guildsmen into entering the forest. You are well aware of the legends that scare them. The Forest of Fernmost was once part of the ancient nation of Taklakot. Beyond the western edge of Fernmost lie the Mountains of Morn, which overlook the infamous 'deadlands'. There stands the forbidden city of Gyanima and the blasted wasteland of Desolation Valley, which was the heart of the kingdom. Centuries ago, Shasarak came to the people of Taklakot as a wise Shianti, though he had turned from the path of goodness long before, refusing the exile that the goddess Ishir had demanded of his people. Because of the forbidden secrets that he unlocked for the race of Taklakot, a great calamity befell them. Great fires rushed through the kingdom and destroyed an entire civilization in a day. Only Shasarak survived, though he was horribly crippled and burnt. Many say that the dead spirits of Taklakot roam the forest of Fernmost to this day, seeking vengeance and taking it upon any who enter the forest.

Samu's words and example seem to work. Gradually the Guildsmen move forward towards the forest. At last all are following the broad trail east, deep into the gloom of the forest. You lead the army into the deepening shadow. The forest shelters an eerie feeling of malice. A grey mist lingers upon the ground and the branches and leaves above form a sombre, green canopy that blots out the sky. There is a strange musty smell in the air. The army are ordered into various positions along the forest's edge to watch for the advance of the Shadakine host you left at the River Dosar. They are completely hidden by the tangled woods and thick undergrowth. Sado tells you he is grateful that you did not ask the army to journey any further into Fernmost, for, as you draw closer to its heart, a strange, watchful presence can be felt.

With a delighted cry you notice clumps of Laumspur, a healing herb, growing in abundance. You chew on the herb and its goodness restores 4 ENDURANCE points. You may store another clump of Laumspur in your Backpack: it will restore 4 ENDURANCE points when chewed.

If you have the Magical Power of Alchemy, turn to **336**.

If you have the Magical Power of Theurgy, turn to **331**.

If you do not have either of these Magical Powers, turn to **300**.

### 313

You are coming to realize the impossible situation you have placed yourself in. You must try another tactic if you are to see the sun set on this day.

Turn to **226**.

### 314

Using 1 WILLPOWER point you call on the elementals for their aid. After a few moments, a huge wave rushes along the river. You and the Masbaté turn and run from the bridge. You look back to see the gigantic wave engulf the bridge, smashing its stones into pebbles and washing the bridge downstream.

Turn to **75**.

### 315

You try to increase your speed but you are almost breathless with exhaustion already. The three howling reptile creatures reach out and drag you to the ground. You manage to beat them off but it is to no avail, for the demonic pack has now reached you. They tear you to pieces.

Your adventure ends here.

### 316 – *Illustration XVII*

You look upon Shasarak's broken features for the last time. The wall of fire is a portal to Agarash's realm. His bargain is to take Agarash's place, to be named ever after as Shasarak the Damned, and to set the demon free. The Wytch-king prefers eternal torment to the peace of death at your hands. Shasarak disappears through the wall and you hurl the shining

XVII.   Shasarak steps through the flaming portal to a realm of
eternal torment

luminescence of the Moonstone at the portal. A huge shoulder and a splayed, clawed foot emerge as you assault the wall.

'No, you cannot . .' the demon lord splutters in fury.

You battle with the power of the demon as it struggles to escape, and throw the last of your WILLPOWER and ENDURANCE at the flames. You must close the portal! Flames rage around the hall, struggling against the purity of the Moonstone's light. A great, yawning blackness threatens to engulf you as a hurricane of might whirls from the Moonstone and assaults the portal. You drop to your knees. You look up once more into the raging war of incandescence before slipping into unconscious oblivion.

Turn to **360**.


## 317

Taking careful aim, you release a searing ball of flame into the heavens and the leader of the fomation falls to the earth, screaming. This attack has cost you 2 WILLPOWER points. The formation becomes disrupted and confused. An ape-like creature swoops towards you. You cannot evade combat.

Winged Demon: COMBAT SKILL 20    ENDURANCE 19

Combat last for one round only as the creature hurtles past. If the Winged Demon loses more ENDURANCE points than you, ignore any ENDURANCE points you lose.

If you are still alive, turn to **287**.

## 318

The Shadakine horseman rushes up the hill towards you. You raise your Staff and aim, attempting to shake the weariness that dulls your vision and causes you to totter.

Pick a number from the *Random Number Table*. Then add the number you have picked to your combined WILLPOWER and ENDURANCE point totals.

If your total is *25* or more, turn to **220**.
If it is less than *25*, turn to **173**.

## 319

Eventually you defeat your grotesque adversaries but it is too late! While you fought, the demon horde has reached you: you suffer a terrible death at their hands.

Your adventure ends here.

## 320

Shasarak screeches as the light of the blazing Moonstone shines on him. His body writhes and he clutches himself in pain as he topples to the floor. He is still. The light of the Moonstone fades and you stoop over the body. As you do so, Shasarak suddenly twists around and sends a bolt of black fire shooting towards you from one crooked fingertip.

If you wish to try to kock aside the blast with the Moonstone, turn to **334**.
If you wish to strike Shasarak with your Staff, turn to **125**

## 321

The night passes without incident and the following morning you and the Masbaté break camp and continue south. You cross a flat land of farms and small villages, the inhabitants of which come out of their homes and look upon you with wonder.

You warn the people of the vast Shadakine Army that follows and that may have already crossed the River Dosar. Though you are glad to see that your presence has heartened so many, you realize with regret that word of your passing is sure to reach the city of Andui to the north east, where there is sure to be a Shadakine garrison. Perhaps it will be sent against you, ahead of the large army trapped north of the River Dosar or perhaps the Shadakine Wytch of that city, Mother Chowloon, sister of Mother Magri of Suhn, will come against you.

Thoughts of Shadakine Wytches remind you of Tanith's plight. You wonder how she fares and whether Mother Magri has successfully drawn Tanith back to the Port of Suhn in the east.

> If you are versed in the higher magick of a Visionary, and wish to exert 2 WILLPOWER points to discover how Tanith is, turn to **305**.
> If not, turn to **282**.

## 322

You hurl every last drop of your power at the demon but it is not enough. He is a demon lord, possessing power beyond your wildest imaginings. At first he hesitates, but, seeing that you have used the last of your power, he reaches out and takes you by the neck and hurls you into the wall of fire, through the fiery portal and into the realm of damnation to join Shasarak in an eternity of flame and torment.

Your quest ends here.

## 323

You must fight Shasarak without the protection of the Moonstone. He has been weakened but by how much you cannot tell. With desperation, you charge at him. His one, hideous eye burns with poisonous malice; his ruined face is twisted with hate.

Turn to **345**.

## 324

At the cost of 2 WILLPOWER points you unleash a bolt of energy at the spearman. He falls, wide-eyed, to the ground in a plume of smoke. Suddenly Samu is at your side. 'Your aim is true,' he comments before lifting his war horn and trumpeting a loud call to arms.

Turn to **347**.

## 325

'Go now,' you call to Sado and his men. 'I will face them.'

The soldiers do as they are asked and you turn to face the chariots thundering across the flat ground before the rise. The Shadakine inside the chariots are still entranced by your spell and the vehicles are veering crazily. One crashes into another, destroying both. Satisfied that your spell has been successful, you turn and make to leave the rise. As you do so, a chariot suddenly swerves out of control and heads towards you. The steel blades of its wheels glitter menacingly.

If you wish to fire a long-range attack at the chariot, and have 2 WILLPOWER points, turn to **303**.

If you prefer to stand and face the chariot, turn to **263**.

If you wish to try to dive out of the swerving course of the chariot, turn to **259**.


### 326

'Alas, Grey Star, there is not time for more. The bridge we have created weakens now. Step warily, for the land is beset with dangers, though there are friends there also, friends you would not expect to see . . .'

With these words, his voice fades completely. You pray that the Shianti have conserved enough energy to transport you back to the real world.

Turn to **50**.


### 327

At the cost of 2 WILLPOWER points you issue a word of command to the ranks of Shadakine warriors and charioteers that head towards you. The warriors stop dead in their tracks, mesmerized by this powerful spell. The Shadakine in the chariots are similarly affected but their progress is not halted as their horses do not respond to this form of magic.

If you wish to stand and face the chariots as they approach, turn to **325**.

If you wish to return to the main army group of the
    Freedom Guild and lead them into the Forest of
    Fernmost, turn to **343**.

**328** – *Illustration XVIII (overleaf)*

You speak your mind to Sado and for once he does
not argue. You mount and you and Samu ride either
side of the grim-faced leader of the Freedom Guild.
Sado gives the command and the entire army surges
forward in pursuit of the ghostly figure of the Kazim as
it heads purposefully into the night.

The battle that follows is long and terrible. The Freedom Guild almost fail but with Sado's iron leadership
and your brave resolve they endure, although the
number of casualties is high. The Kazim reclaims its
heart of stone, slaying Mother Chowloon, the
Shadakine Wytch who bore it. As she dies, much of
the fighting fury and ferocity that filled the Shadakine,
fades. The Army of the Freedom Guild senses the
Shadakine's loss of morale and press home their
advantage. Soon, they have beaten the much larger
force into a full-scale retreat. The entire Shadkine
Army heads north. Sado leads his army in pursuit,
turning the retreat into a rout. It is vital that the
Shadakine Army does not reach Shadaki, for there
they would find new leadership under Shasarak's
hand. They are still a large army and with Shasarak to
lead them they could turn the tables once again.

The Army of the Freedom Guild pursues the fleeing
Shadakine Army across much of the Shadakine
Empire. The Shadakine find no place to hide, for all
the cities of the Empire are in open revolt. Each
Kazim has reclaimed its heart and slain the Shadakine

XVIII.   The Freedom Guild surges forward, the ghostly figure of
Kazim leading the way

Wytch that ruled each city. During the four days of the pursuit you are not required to exert any energy or use any of your Magical Powers and you regain 8 ENDURANCE points and 9 WILLPOWER points. Constantly harrying the ever-dwindling Shadakine force, the Army of the Freedom Guild crosses the great Kalamar River and approaches the Mountains of Lara.

The Mountains of Lara contain the infamous Morn Pass. It was through this pass that the Shadakine first invaded the provinces of the south. It is the last barrier between you and the fortress city of Shadaki. With growing dread you realize that the time of your final battle with Shasarak is fast approaching. With his armies scattered or destroyed, it only remains for you to challenge him yourself and ensure that the land remains free. Your trepidation is coupled with suspicion. Shasarak has many powers at his disposal. Why then has he not used them to challenge Sado's tiny army, much reduced in numbers? Perhaps there is some other reason why he does not bring his full might to bear?

> If you are versed in the higher magick of Thaumaturgy, possess a Temeris Potion, or wish to use the Dimension Door of the Moonstone to teleport into the city of Shadaki and challenge Shasarak now, turn to **191**.

> If you wish to continue with the Army of the Freedom Guild through the Morn Pass, turn to **342**.

## 329

When you reach the camp, you see that the army has

been delayed; not by the difficulty of moving such a large group of men quickly, but because of the Forest of Fernmost itself. Many of the Guildsmen regard it with dread, muttering darkly among themselves.

Turn to **312**.

## 330

The warrior stops and releases his spear like a javelin, aimed at your heart. Suddenly Samu knocks you to the ground. He has saved your life.

Turn to **347**.

## 331

Your trained eye quickly perceives that many unusual plants grow in the forest, some of which are of immense use to your Theurgical powers. The army is well equipped and you are able to borrow many vials from a healer. While Sado and his men watch for the approach of the Shadakine Army, you pass the day searching for various herbs and preparing potions. It is evening by the time you have finished. You have the choice of making and keeping any of the following items for future use. Remember that your Herb Pouch can hold up to six items, and any other potions may be stored in your Backpack.

- 2 Potions of Laumspur (Each Potion restores up to 6 ENDURANCE points when swallowed before or after combat. One potion equals one dose.)
- 1 Potion of Alether (Increases COMBAT SKILL by 2 points when swallowed before an attack.)
- 2 Tamara Seeds (Swallowing one seed enables a wizard to use his Wizard's Staff or Magical

Power without losing any WILLPOWER points.
They take up no room in your Herb Pouch or
Backpack.)

1 Calacena Potion (A useful aid to the casting of
spells of Enchantment.)

1 Potion of Mustow (Creates a foul, choking gas.)

1 Potion of Temeris (Allows a wizard to teleport to
any place he desires.)

1 Potion of Ezeran Acid (A metal-eating acid.)

If you have some Phinomel pods, turn to **355**.
If not, turn to **359**.

### 332

At the cost of 1 WILLPOWER point you summon a wind
of your own design. It blows through the tree-tops of
the Forest of Fernmost and sends the dense cloud
above swirling across the sky. The cloud disperses to
reveal the moon once more.

'My thanks,' Sado says with a grin. You turn your
attention to the Shadakine Army once more.

Turn to **230**.

### 333

You call on your own elemental powers and, at the
cost of 2 WILLPOWER points, concentrate on a stretch of
flat land that lies in the path of the oncoming chariots.
At first nothing happens. Then the earth trembles and
small cracks appear in the ground. Stones crumble
and the chariot horses of the Shadakine neigh with
fright. A low rumbling sounds from below the ground.

'Away!' you cry to Sado and his men. 'My work is done
here. The Shadakine are doomed.'

The soldiers do as they are commanded. Suddenly a vast chasm opens in the land. The Shadakine scream as they are swallowed by the pit, falling to their deaths far below. You and the men of the Freedom Guild leave the rise and go to rejoin the main army.

Turn to **329**.

## 334

The blast is totally absorbed by the Moonstone but its light is extinguished. Shasarak screams at you like a caged animal. He climbs to his feet, his Staff held high, ready to attack. You bring up your own Staff to fend off the blow you know must come.

Turn to **323**.

## 335

You turn and run from the warrior, who stops and throws his spear. It thuds into your back and you drop to your knees, crying out in pain before falling face-down in the dirt.

Your life and your adventure end here.

## 336

Your Alchemist's eye tells you that many unusual plants grow in the forest, some of which are of great use. You borrow some empty vials from a healer in the army's employ. While Sado and his men watch for the approach of the Shadakine Army, you pass the day searching for various herbs and plants and preparing potions. It is evening by the time you have finished. You have the choice of making and keeping any of the following items for future use. Remember that your Herb Pouch will hold up to six items may be stored in your Backpack.

2 Potions of Laumspur (Each Potion restores up to 6 ENDURANCE points when swallowed before or after combat. One potion equals one dose.)

1 Potion of Alether (Increases COMBAT SKILL by 2 points when swallowed before an attack.)

2 Tamara Seeds (Swallowing one seed enables a wizard to use his Wizard's Staff or Magical Power without losing any WILLPOWER points. They take up no room in your Herb Pouch or Backpack.)

1 Calacena Potion (A useful aid to the casting of spells of Enchantment.)

1 Potion of Mustow (Creates a foul, choking gas.)

1 Potion of Ezeran Acid (A metal-eating acid.)

If you have some Phinomel pods, turn to **355**.
If not, turn to **359**.

## 337

You mount and ride with all speed to the site of the battle at the northern edge of the camp. You arrive to see Sado with a hundred cavalry upon a low rise overlooking the battle. As many as a thousand Shadakine foot soldiers are charging towards you.

'Good morning to you Grey Star,' Sado calls. 'The morning begins with battle. Have a care to stay by me, for you know not the strategy I have in mind and you must be sure to move when I do.'

You glance behind the line of Sado's cavalrymen and see a line of soldiers armed with crossbows, busily loading their weapons. The warriors are kneeling to conceal their presence. When the Shadakine have drawn but two hundred paces away, Sado barks a command. At his word, the line of horsemen parts to allow those bearing crossbows to step forward. Sado shouts again and the crossbowmen release a deadly hail of arrows that fly towards the Shadakine host. Many fall dead in the face of this lethal volley. But incredibly the survivors continue.

'These Shadakine are strong of heart. Brave but foolish,' Sado murmurs.

The crossbowmen reload and release another shower of arrows. As the bolts find their targets, many more Shadakine fall dead. More than half their number have now fallen. You look back to the camp: it is still a chaotic mass of rushing men, trying to order themselves and leave. Samu and his Masbaté have already left in good order but they have the advantage of smaller numbers and a strong leader to command them.

The Shadakine continue to advance, their faces set with grim determination. There is no time for the crossbowmen to reload their weapons before the remainder of the Shadakine, almost five hundred men, fall upon the Guild's ranks. At Sado's command, the cavalry charges down the rise at the Shadakine. A furious melée ensues but the Shadakine maintain the upper hand and the cavalry are forced to retreat in disorder. It will not be long before the Shadakine are fighting against the bulk of the army of the Freedom Guild, who are still attempting to flee into the forest. Looking to the distant hills, you see the reason for this early raid by the Shadakine. A line of Shadakine chariots has appeared. From earlier encounters with the Shadakine, you know that sharpened blades adorn the wheels of the chariots. You shudder to think of the harm they could inflict on the disordered lines of the retiring Freedom Guild.

If you wish to lead the main army group of the Freedom Guild into the forest of Fernmost, turn to **343**.

If you are versed in the higher magick of Physiurgy, and wish to expend 2 WILLPOWER points using it against the chariots of the Shadakine, turn to **333**.

If you are versed on the higher magick of Telergy and wish to expend 2 WILLPOWER points using it against the Shadakine, turn to **327**.

### 338

You go into a trance state, calling to the elemental plane for aid. You tell the elemental spirits that dwell there of your need for light. Deduct 2 WILLPOWER points for your use of this Magical Power.

If you wish for the aid of the element of earth, turn to **120**.

If you wish for the aid of the element of water, turn to **138**.

If you wish for the aid of the element of air, turn to **341**.

If you wish for the aid of the element of fire, turn to **349**.

### 339

Overcoming your fear you charge, your Staff exploding into flame. The tall shapes are towering rocks with stony faces resembling humans'. You cast magical flames at all seven of the stone creatures in a frenzy of energy, but the attack has no effect. With a great roar, you are assaulted on all sides by a terrible force that seizes your brain. You are flung into a deep, dark void from which you never return.

Your life and your quest end here.

## 340

'This shall be done,' comes the reply. 'Look into the Moonstone and your wish shall be granted.'

You obey and gaze into the stone. Gradually the colour of the stone begins to change. It darkens until it contains a grey mist. The heart of the mist clears and a hazy image appears. You are looking upon a huge, grim city that overlooks the sea. Its looming walls are built of black stone and granite from the mountains of Jazer. The image shifts and you feel as if you are being drawn into the city with its tall, crenellated walls and towers. You guess that this is the fortress city of Shadaki, Shasarak's home, and the heart of the Shadakine Empire. The scene shifts to a high tower, and suddenly you are looking down into a wide, round hall, full of darkness and forboding. At one end of the hall is a throne, rudely carved from stone; at the other end is a wall of fire. Kneeling before the wall of fire is the crippled figure of Shasarak, who looks as if he is pleading with someone. A pair of eyes stares out from the wall of fire. Suddenly the picture fades.

Turn to **326**.

## 341

A strong wind begins to blow. The dense cloud in the sky begins to move and soon the moon is revealed once more.

'This is your doing?' asks Sado, amazed.

You nod, blushing with pride, and return your attention to the Shadakine Army.

Turn to **230**.

### 342 – *Illustration XIX (overleaf)*

You come to the Morn Pass and cautiously enter the long, barren trail that runs between the mountains. Your senses scream a warning at you; every nerve is taut. Looking down, you see that the Moonstone has turned black and you sense a terrible evil, sorcerous in nature. The hairs on the back of your neck rise and your blood runs like ice in your veins. Ignorant of the torment you suffer, Sado looks over to you, a broad smile splitting his face. His eyes shine with the joy of his victory over the Shadakine. If only he knew what it is you must yet face. You hope his confidence in you is not misplaced.

A faint tremor shakes the ground. Horses rear and whinny their distress as the land cracks and splits. All eyes look in horror at the shapes now heaving out of the ground, twisting blindly with skeletal claws outstretched. Humans, horses, all manner of beasts, crawl out into the light from their graves beneath the pass. Shasarak, the master Necromancer, has summoned the legions of the dead that lie beneath this old battlefield. Hundreds of gnarled shapes rise up, blocking each end of the pass. The army is

XIX.   The twisted shapes of the undead heave up from the cracked earth

trapped and you with it. A skeleton shape stands before you, its frozen smile leering savagely. It has a rusty sword in its hand and leans forward to strike.

Skeleton Warrior: COMBAT SKILL 20     ENDURANCE 25

If you win the combat, turn to **12**.

### 343

You ride among the army camp, calling to all. 'Follow, follow. We go to the Fernmost. I will lead you there. There is nothing to fear.'

Many of the Guildsmen nearby shake their heads. The legends of the forest are steeped in legend and dark mystery and the soldiers are filled with a superstitous fear of it. You look around in desperation, willing someone to follow you.

Turn to **312**.

### 344

The light from your Staff is making you an easy target for Shadakine crossbowmen and you decide that you might be better off without it. The fighting is coming closer.

If you wish to head towards the sound of the fighting, turn to **216**.
If you wish to try to find Sado, turn to **242**.

### 345

Staff clashes against Staff and the hall is filled with flame as you fight. Agarash's unholy joy ripples through the room in peals of mocking laughter, the black, fathomless eyes following every move. You are locked in a duel with your arch enemy.

Wytch-king Shasarak:
COMBAT SKILL 30    ENDURANCE 25

If you win the combat, turn to **180**.

## 346

It is a foolish decision, for the army is forced to advance out of the forest later anyway, with a raging fire at their backs and a ravening horde before them. They are panicky and disordered, and in no state to fight the Shadakine warriors. Though the Kazim retrieves the stone that is its heart and kills the Shadakine Wytch that once owned it, the loss of their leader is not a sufficient blow to their morale to stop the Shadakine from continuing their battle with the Freedom League. The ranks of Sado's men are completely decimated and, though you are the last to fall, you are slain by the triumphant Shadakine horde, and your head is taken to the fortress city of Shadaki as a gift to the Wytch-king, Shasarak.

You have failed in your quest; your adventure ends here.

## 347

With valiant cries, the entire force of the Masbaté tribesmen charges from the forest, running to the aid of Sado, who is beleagured upon the hill. The Masbaté have managed to stay ordered and controlled under Samu's command, despite the surprise of the Shadakine night attack, and their charge is ferocious and deadly. The Shadakine are swept back and away from the hill. Soon they have fallen into a full retreat and the men of the Freedom Guild give a loud cheer.

While Sado organizes his men into battle formations, and sends couriers dashing through the forest with messages for the rest of the army, you stare out at the Shadakine host, trying to guess their next move. A cloud drifts across the moon's face, blotting out its silver light and plunging you into darkness once more. Sado curses. 'Grey Star, is there nothing you can do to bring us light?' he asks.

'I cannot command the sun to rise before dawn,' you reply bitterly. If only there were some way of fulfilling Sado's request. You are also anxious to see the movements of the Shadakine.

> If you possess the Magical Power of Elementalism, and wish to use it, expending 2 WILLPOWER points, turn to **338**.
> If you are versed in the higher magick of Physiurgy, and wish to expend 1 WILLPOWER point using it, turn to **332**.
> If you do not have either of these Magical Powers, or do not wish to use them, turn to **275**.

### 348

'We are only able to send you to the Lissan Plain, the north-western province of the Shadakine Empire (see the map at the beginning of the book). This was once the domain of the Masbaté tribe, warrior nomads of great prowess and strength. It was Shasarak who brought doom to these once-great people, when the Shadakine Empire was first won. In a terrible war, hordes of Shadakine warriors pursued the Masbaté across the plains in their great war chariots, led by the Wytch-king himself. The Masbaté were able to resist the Shadakine, despite overwhelming odds, until Shasarak summoned the demon plague. Faced with such an assault, the Masbaté were unable to resist and an entire race was wiped from the face of the world. The demons still roam the plains, and no one dares go there. The vast expanse of the Lissan Plain was once rich and fertile. Now, none may benefit from it, save for the scavenging packs of hell beasts that roam there.'

His voice has begun to grow very faint.

Turn to **326**.

## 349

Your call for aid is answered by the element of fire in the only way it is able. Sheets of flame spring up all around you, catching the dry brush and foliage of the forest in seconds. The bright light of the fires provides an excellent target for the Shadakine crossbowmen. A hail of arrows arcs towards you.

Your life and your quest end here.

## 350

Shasarak's torment is written in deep lines upon his ruined face. The wall of fire is a portal to Agarash's realm. Shasarak's bargain is to change places with Agarash, setting the demon free and enduring Agarash's banishment for all time. He chooses eternal torment before eternal death.

As Shasarak disappears through the wall, Agarash

calls out with glee, 'Free, free at last!' The eyes disappear and a vast, flaming shoulder moves out from the wall. You glimpse a wing and a clawed foot.

If you wish to use the last of your WILLPOWER and ENDURANCE points to attack the demon lord as he steps through the portal, turn to **322**.

If you wish to use the last of your WILLPOWER and ENDURANCE points to attempt to close the portal, turn to **356**.

### 351

A feeling of panic surges through the men. Sado looks aghast. The army will be forced out of the forest and into the jaws of the Shadakine to be slaughtered, for the Freedom Guild lacks sufficient numbers to face the Shadakine in an all-out assault. Just as you think you are facing certain doom, a vast shape immersed in a pallid, yellow glow strides out from amongst the burning trees. It is a Kazim. Many of Sado's men shout out in alarm and horror, thinking that they are being attacked from the rear but you know this is not the case.

'Do not worry,' you assure Sado. 'This is a Kazim. It fights with us.'

The stony creature, measuring twelve feet high at least, moves through the parting ranks of Guildsmen and stops at the edge of the forest. It is alone; the other Kazim must already be on their way to the other Shadakine Wytches in the pursuit of their hearts. The Kazim at the edge of the forest turns its head this way and that, searching. When it has located that which it seeks, it moves forward at great speed.

If you wish to tell Sado to command his army to
   follow the Kazim, turn to **328**.

If you wish to remain in the forest, turn to **346**.

### 352 – *Illustration XX*

Your horse quickly covers the miles of your long,
desperate ride. The demon host has not caught you,
although it is not far away. Looking to the east you
see great clouds of dust hanging in the air. These are
the tell-tale signs of an army on the move. It must be
the rear of the Shadakine column approaching the
bridge at Lanzi. You double your speed. Now you
can hear the cries of battle and the ringing of steel.
You gallop around the edge of the town of Lanzi on
its western side and emerge close to the River Dosar.
Reining in the horse for a moment, you stop and look
along the line of the river. A mile away you can see
the bridge. The Masbaté still hold it but they fight a
desperate battle against a huge force of Shadakine
warriors.

With a wild yell, you head towards the battle, the
demon pack baying at your heels. You reach the
Shadakine force that fights at the bridge and, rushing
up to an officer, you indicate the demon horde
behind you. He curses and orders some of his men to
turn and face this new threat. He orders you to the
rear of the army group. 'Alert Warward Gatakhan,'
he shouts after you. 'He must bring forward more
men.'

You nod your head, although, of course, you have
no intention of obeying the order. Your sole objective
is to cross the river and tell the Masbaté that they may
join the Army of the Freedom Guild in the south.

XX. The Masbaté fight a desperate battle against a huge force of Shadakine

If you are versed in the higher magick of Thaumaturgy, and wish to use it to teleport across the river and have 2 WILLPOWER points, turn to **195**.

If you wish to try to swim across the river, turn to **238**.

If you wish to try to fight your way across the bridge, turn to **256**.

## 353

In a stunning display of battle skills, you hack a path of blazing, magical fire through the Shadakine ranks. On the bridge you can hear the cheering of the Masbaté as you wreak terrible havoc among your foes. They urge you on, their cries growing louder as you draw nearer. Suddenly your horse is cut from under you and you throw yourself clear and on to the stone bridge to run the last - steps towards the Masbaté. They rush forward to protect your flanks. You are safe. Samu rushes to meet you. 'Grey Star, that was magnificent . . . ' he begins.

'No time . . . no time,' you pant. 'Sound the retreat. We must flee. See? I have brought the demon plague.'

It is as you say. Even now, across the river, you can see a wild, screaming mass as the demon horde battles with the Shadakine. Samu nods and springs into action. He sounds a battle horn and the Masbaté retire. The Shadakine cannot pursue while the demon host fights at their back. However, you must destroy the bridge to prevent pursuit should the Shadakine, whose entire army numbers in thousands defeat the demon plague too soon.

If you have the Magical Power of Elementalism, and wish to use it, turn to **314**.

If you are versed in the higher magick of Physiurgy, and wish to use it, turn to **7**.

If you are versed in the higher magick of Thaumaturgy, and wish to use it, turn to **26**.

## 354

Dawn is breaking when the alarm is raised and you are alerted to an attack on the camp. Swiftly you rise, taking up your Staff and rushing outside. There is great clamour everywhere. Men are rushing in all directions, still donning their armour. You rush towards Sado's tent. He is not there but an attendant tells you that a group of Shadakine has attempted an attack. Sado is already at the scene of the battle with a unit of soldiers, hand picked to fight a rearguard action, while the remainder of the army retreats to the Forest of Fernmost. This unit was chosen by Sado himself last night in readiness for just such an eventuality. You are sure that the Shadakine attack cannot be from the large army you trapped on the other side of the River Dosar; it can only be the garrison from Andui.

If you wish to go to the scene of the battle, where Sado fights a rearguard action, turn to **337**.

If you wish to lead the bulk of the army into the Forest of Fernmost, turn to **343**.

## 355

You see a deep pool of greenish liquid called Leafwater, a strange and unique plant. When Phinomel pods are cast into the pool the watery substance is transformed. For every pod you cast into it, add 1 to your COMBAT SKILL when you dip a weapon into it. You may affect your Wizard's Staff in this way.

Turn to **359**.

## 356

You hurl the fury of your last desperate attack at the portal, attempting to close it.

'NO!' the demon thunders. 'Do not . . .'

You battle on as the demon struggles to escape with all its power. You must close the portal and tear down the wall. Flame rages around the hall, striving against the purity of the Moonstone's light. A yawning blackness threatens to engulf you as a hurricane of might swirls out from the Moonstone and assaults the portal, a doorway to damnation. You fall to your knees and look up into the raging wall of incandescence before slipping into unconsciousness.

Turn to **360**.

## 357

You are seen by a group of Shadakine crossbowmen and, as the only bearer of light for miles around, present an easy target. Before you can move again, another hail of arrows flies towards you. This time their aim is better. You fall to the ground, a mass of feathered shafts protruding from your body.

Your life and your quest end here.

## 358

With all the speed you can muster, you rush towards the fray. When you arrive, all is in darkness and confusion. You hear swords clashing in the shadows at the edge of the forest but you cannot see who is fighting whom.

If you wish to expend 1 WILLPOWER point to cast a light with your Staff, turn to **157**.

If you wish to head towards the sound of the fighting, turn to **216**.

If you wish to continue through the forest and try to find Sado, turn to **242**.

## 359

You return to the army laden with useful aids for your struggle. They seem to be more relaxed about the Forest of Fernmost, although you still sense a strange presence somewhere in the centre of the forest.

Turn to **300**.

## 360

You wake to see the face of Tanith looking into yours. You sit up with a jolt. You are lying in a bed in a tall tower. 'The portal . . . Agarash . . . is he . . . ?' you stammer.

Tanith smiles. 'All vanquished,' she replies. 'The demon lord, Agarash and his portal of fire have gone and Shasarak with them. You have triumphed, Grey Star. We are saved.'

With a wild laugh you leap from the bed and hug Tanith with joy. You have saved your people.

'Come,' she says, leading you to a doorway. It opens on to a balcony that overlooks a large square in the centre of the city of Shadaki. There you look upon a huge crowd. They let out a thunderous cheer as they see you.

Later you retire to the chamber. Standing there are Sado of the Long Knife and Samu, the Masbaté King. You clasp their outstretched hands, eyes brimming with tears of happiness. You grin furiously, glad to see that they are alive. A wave of exultant relief runs through you as you receive their grateful thanks and congratulations. They tell you that the Shadakine have fled back to the Sadi Desert. All the cities of the land are free capitals as before. The long task of rebuilding has already begun and all sing your praise to the furthest corners of what was once the Shadakine Empire. They have proclaimed you their ruler, the Wizard Regent of the Free Peoples, for their faith and trust in your wisdom and courage is unshakable.

Hail! Wizard Grey Star, Shianti Hero and Saviour.

# FOR THE ULTIMATE SWORD-AND-SORCERY ADVENTURE STEP INTO THE WORLD OF MAGNAMUND!

# THE MAGNAMUND COMPANION

### The Complete Guide to the World of *Lone Wolf* and *Grey Star*

A fully illustrated guide to the fantastic world of Magnamund — with beautifully detailed maps, full-color pictures, and a new solo adventure in which you are the hero.

There's full background detail on all the characters in the Lone Wolf books, as well as exciting history. Oversized paperback.

__THE MAGNAMUND COMPANION
    by Joe Dever and Gary Chalk  0-425-10759-0/$6.95

Don't miss the other *Lone Wolf* and *The World of Lone Wolf* adventures!

---

**Check book(s). Fill out coupon. Send to:**

**BERKLEY PUBLISHING GROUP**
390 Murray Hill Pkwy., Dept. B
East Rutherford, NJ 07073

NAME_____

ADDRESS_____

CITY_____

STATE_____ZIP_____

**PLEASE ALLOW 6 WEEKS FOR DELIVERY.
PRICES ARE SUBJECT TO CHANGE
WITHOUT NOTICE.**

**POSTAGE AND HANDLING:**
$1.00 for one book, 25¢ for each additional. Do not exceed $3.50.

**BOOK TOTAL**                    $ ____

**POSTAGE & HANDLING**     $ ____

**APPLICABLE SALES TAX**     $ ____
(CA, NJ, NY, PA)

**TOTAL AMOUNT DUE**          $ ____

**PAYABLE IN US FUNDS.**
(No cash orders accepted.)

236

# RANDOM NUMBER TABLE

| 1 | 4 | 1 | 3 | 6 | 0 | 5 | 2 | 4 | 4 |
|---|---|---|---|---|---|---|---|---|---|
| 5 | 4 | 1 | 6 | 9 | 7 | 5 | 9 | 7 | 6 |
| 6 | 8 | 2 | 6 | 2 | 3 | 0 | 2 | 5 | 9 |
| 0 | 4 | 8 | 9 | 1 | 1 | 7 | 5 | 2 | 6 |
| 1 | 7 | 3 | 5 | 1 | 9 | 5 | 6 | 5 | 3 |
| 0 | 2 | 8 | 1 | 8 | 2 | 4 | 6 | 0 | 4 |
| 9 | 2 | 7 | 9 | 7 | 0 | 8 | 5 | 4 | 6 |
| 2 | 5 | 6 | 8 | 6 | 2 | 8 | 3 | 6 | 7 |
| 8 | 4 | 0 | 7 | 4 | 1 | 8 | 4 | 9 | 8 |
| 6 | 9 | 0 | 1 | 0 | 5 | 5 | 4 | 0 | 3 |

# COMBAT RULES SUMMARY

1. Calculate your COMBAT SKILL based on the weapon that you are using.

2. Subtract the COMBAT SKILL of your enemy from this total. This number = Combat Ratio.

3. If using your Wizard's Staff, note the number of WILLPOWER points you wish to expend.

4. Turn to *Combat Results Table*.

5. Find your Combat Ratio on the top of chart and cross reference to random number you have picked. (*E* indicates loss of ENDURANCE points to Enemy. *GS* indicates loss of ENDURANCE points to Grey Star.)

6. Multiply the enemy's lost ENDURANCE points by the number of WILLPOWER points used.

7. Continue the combat from Stage 3 until one character is dead. This is when ENDURANCE points of either character fall to 0.

## TO EVADE COMBAT

1. You may only evade combat when the text of the adventure offers you the opportunity.

2. You undertake one round of combat in the usual way. All points lost by the enemy are ignored, only Grey Star loses ENDURANCE points.

3. If the book offers the chance of taking evasive action in place of combat, it can be taken in the first round of combat or any subsequent round.

# COMBAT RE

## Combat Ratio

| Random Number | | −11 OR GREATER | −10/−9 | −8/−7 | −6/−5 | −4/−3 | −2/−1 |
|---|---|---|---|---|---|---|---|
| 1 | E | −0 | −0 | −0 | −0 | −1 | −2 |
|   | GS | K | K | −8 | −6 | −6 | −5 |
| 2 | E | −0 | −0 | −0 | −1 | −2 | −3 |
|   | GS | K | −8 | −7 | −6 | −5 | −5 |
| 3 | E | −0 | −0 | −1 | −2 | −3 | −4 |
|   | GS | −8 | −7 | −6 | −5 | −5 | −4 |
| 4 | E | −0 | −1 | −2 | −3 | −4 | −5 |
|   | GS | −8 | −7 | −6 | −5 | −4 | −4 |
| 5 | E | −1 | −2 | −3 | −4 | −5 | −6 |
|   | GS | −7 | −6 | −5 | −4 | −4 | −3 |
| 6 | E | −2 | −3 | −4 | −5 | −6 | −7 |
|   | GS | −6 | −6 | −5 | −4 | −3 | −2 |
| 7 | E | −3 | −4 | −5 | −6 | −7 | −8 |
|   | GS | −5 | −5 | −4 | −3 | −2 | −2 |
| 8 | E | −4 | −5 | −6 | −7 | −8 | −9 |
|   | GS | −4 | −4 | −3 | −2 | −1 | −1 |
| 9 | E | −5 | −6 | −7 | −8 | −9 | −10 |
|   | GS | −3 | −3 | −2 | −0 | −0 | −0 |
| 0 | E | −6 | −7 | −8 | −9 | −10 | −11 |
|   | GS | −0 | −0 | −0 | −0 | −0 | −0 |

E = ENEMY    GS = GREY STAR